Tessa's Garden

Four Contemporary Novellas

LARGE PRINT VERSION

Tessa's Spring
Tessa's Summer
Tessa's Autumn
Tessa's Winter

J.L. STARR

Impassioned Romance Books

ISBN-13: 978-1542515733

ISBN-10: 1542515734

Independently Published

Other Books by J.L. Starr

Her Makeover

My Chance

The Nanny's Secret

One Simple Thing

From Southern Girl To

Crimson Star

Time For You

Table of Contents

Tessa's Spring...................................1

Tessa's Summer........................127

Tessa's Autumn........................233

Tessa's Winter..........................343

About The Author.....................487

Tessa's Spring

Chapter One

"It's not illegal," Tessa's boss told her. "Everything we're doing is well within the boundaries of the law."

"That doesn't make it right," Tessa said. "I mean, these reports—"

"Those reports are company secrets," Mr. Morgan said. "I trust we have an understanding in that regard? I can't have anyone leaking our internal information."

Tessa held the file folder in her hands, struggling with what was inside. She wasn't sure what to do, though her gut was telling her that there was something very wrong going on at Dunham Enterprises. The nationwide food chain had a reputation for providing clean, wholly organic products, though the more time she spent on the inside, the more Tessa was starting to question what she knew about her employer.

"Are we going to have a problem here?" Mr. Morgan asked. He studied her like he was readying the chopping block.

"No problem, Mr. Morgan," she said. "It's just that I don't want to get myself into any trouble. If I'm liable..."

"Don't worry." He smiled and patted her on the arm. "You won't be held liable for anything. Besides, like I said, everything we're doing is perfectly legal. All the major corporations operate this way."

"They do?"

"Of course. It's the cost of doing business. Perfectly standard."

"Oh." Tessa looked down at the file folder, wondering if she'd simply misunderstood it. "All right. Sorry for taking up so much of your time."

"No problem at all." Mr. Morgan turned to leave, then paused and looked back at her. "I'm glad you brought this to my attention first, Tessa. You're a smart girl. I've always thought you do an excellent job here. You probably know that if internal information were ever leaked to the press, it could cause a scandal. That's the sort of thing that costs people their jobs. I'm sure you don't want that."

"No," Tessa said. "I definitely don't."

"Good."

Mr. Morgan left, and Tessa returned to her cubicle. She sat in her chair, her shoulders slumped, and tossed the folder onto her desk.

A head topped with short, spiky read hair popped up over the wall of her cubicle. "What was that all about?"

Mindy asked. She glanced down at Tessa, then looked over the wall at Mr. Morgan as he headed out the office door.

"Nothing," Tessa said, keeping her head down. "I don't want to talk about it."

Mindy leaned her arms on the wall and peered down at her. "You okay, Tess? You've been pent up all day."

Tessa tapped her fingers on the folder in front of her. She opened her mouth to say something, then remembered what Mr. Morgan had said about not letting certain things be spread. "It's nothing. I'm just having a rough day. I can't wait to get finished here, go home, pop open a bottle of wine, and get my hands dirty."

Mindy snorted and shook her head. "Okay then, if you say so." She disappeared back into her own cubicle, leaving Tessa alone with her work.

She booted up her computer and navigated through the company's archaic online file system until she found the folders she needed. This was supposed to be the easy part of her work. Tessa's department at Dunham was responsible for organizing inventory reports, results from health inspections, and internal safety test reports, all gathered from the hundreds of manufacturing branches the company had around the country. There was an endless stream of files and reports coming into the office. So many files, in fact, that there was a three year backlog on getting them entered into the system. There were stacks upon stacks of boxes lined up along the wall on one side of the office, containing all of the files that needed to be organized, typed up, investigated, and eventually disposed of.

Tessa started entering the information from the report into the online database. It was a tedious process, mostly consisting of typing in the handwritten notes made by plant managers and inspectors. The company handled a lot of things digitally, but with a corporation this size, there was simply no way to avoid good old fashioned paperwork for some of the most mundane, grueling tasks.

As she entered the information from the report, Tessa tried not to think about the meaning behind it. She didn't know much about how pesticides and Genetically Modified Organisms worked, but Dunham Enterprises always advertised its products as being completely natural and organic. The report showed that a number of GMOs were used in the ingredients of a large number of Dunham's products, and that there were traces of some potentially harmful pesticides. The man who'd written the report, one of Dunham's own internal Quality Assurance Inspectors, had made a note in his report suggesting further investigation.

Tessa finished entering the

information into the computer, hit "SUBMIT," then placed the folder in her outbox with the rest of the files she'd gone through that day. It was getting close to 5:00, so she grabbed her stack of folders and headed for the shredding room.

There were several large, industrial-size cross-cut paper shredders standing throughout the room, each one with a waste bin packed with little confetti-sized bits of paper. The janitor, Corey, was already there dumping the contents of the bins into large plastic bags and loading them into a trash cart to be hauled off for recycling.

"Hey there, Tessa," he said, nodding to her. "I haven't dumped number three yet, you can use that one."

"Thanks," Tessa said. She set the stack of folders on the side of the machine and started pulling out any staples she found so they wouldn't jam up the shredder. Bits of paper snowed down into the waste bin in a steady stream as she fed the files in one after another.

She saved the file on the GMOs for last. She tapped her fingers against it, considering something stupid and possibly dangerous. She didn't want to get anyone in trouble, and she really didn't want to lose her job. It would could cost a *lot* of people their jobs if this information got leaked.

But on the other hand, she thought about all the people who could potentially get sick if they didn't realize what they were eating. She didn't believe that all GMOs were automatically dangerous, but if there was even the possibility, she could end up responsible for a lot of suffering.

Tessa chewed on her lip until the other files finished shredding and the snowfall into the waste bin stopped. Then she tucked the last remaining folder under her jacket and turned to leave.

"Tessa?" Corey said.

She stopped and glanced back over her shoulder.

"You have yourself a good night," he said, nodding to her.

"Thanks. You too."

She hurried from the room, stopping at her desk to get her purse. She folded the file in half and shoved it into her purse, then headed out the door, feeling eyes on her back the entire time.

Chapter Two

When she got home, Tessa pulled out the stolen file folder and stared at it. She wasn't sure why she'd taken it. She had no idea what to do with it. It had just seemed like the thing to do.

Thinking about the consequences set her on edge. She licked her lips and looked around her apartment, then shoved the folder in her desk drawer and tried to forget about it. She wiped her hands on her shirt, pacing around the room. Without any ideas about what she was supposed to do, or if she should even do anything at all, she decided she needed some stress relief. Something to keep her hands and her mind busy.

She changed out of her work clothes and into jeans and an old, worn shirt.

She grabbed her gardening caddy off the counter and headed out the back door, to the broad community gardening plot that sat between the apartment buildings.

The plot was huge, stretching out behind her apartment building all the way up to the next building across the way. It had been divided into several dozen patches, each "owned" by a different tenant. Tessa wasn't sure how the community gardening plot had gotten started; she'd inherited her small plot when she'd moved in, taking over the space that had belonged to the previous tenant. Tending her garden had become her hobby and her stress relief. Plus it was nice to have fresh-grown produce throughout the warmer parts of the year. Most of the tenants traded fruits and vegetables with each other, so while Tessa mostly grew tomatoes and watermelons, she always had plenty of fresh berries, carrots, and other produce given to her by her neighbors.

She greeted a few of her neighbors on her way to her part of the patch. It was a nice, sunny day outside, so there were several people out tending their gardens. She said hello to an older woman who grew flowers in her plot, and an Asian couple who had a little koi pond in the corner of their plot. Everyone grew something different, and the only rule was that everything had to be all-natural. There were no chemical fertilizers, no artificial products. Just a patchwork field covered in little plots of nature.

Tessa pulled on her gloves and got to work digging up the soil and mixing in organic fertilizer she bought from a local supplier. It was early in the season yet, and her plot was mostly an empty patch of dirt for now. She needed to fertilize the soil after the long, dry winter, and loosen the dirt to give the roots plenty of room to grow and thrive. She planted several tall trellises in the ground around the patch, to give the tomato plants somewhere to grow. They would help keep the tomatoes off the ground, keeping them cleaner and easier to inspect and harvest.

She was working up a pretty good sweat when the ringing of a bicycle bell announced the arrival of her neighbor, Samson. He pedaled his bike around the back of the apartment building and stopped not far from her. He pulled a wooden case of herb seedlings from the basket hanging from the handlebars, then brought it over to his plot, right next to Tessa's. His garden was a busy, crowded patch, with vegetables growing in the soil, and benches lining the area, each covered in collections of clay plots for his herbs.

"Good afternoon, Tessa," he said, flashing her a smile. He had long blond hair pulled back in a ponytail, and he had a style that could only be described as "hipster hippie." He wore skinny jeans and a loose flannel shirt over a tight tie-dyed t-shirt. Sometimes Tessa thought he belonged back in the sixties, but the iPod in his pocket marked him as a millennial through and through.

"Hey, Samson." She waved at him, scattering specks of dirt from her gloves.

"How's life treating you?" He set the box of herb seedlings on one of his benches and started sorting through them. He dumped some of the old, dry dirt from the clay pots on the bench and refilled them with fresh soil to help the new herbs thrive.

"I'm not even sure how to answer that question anymore." She lowered her head, trying to focus on her work. She hacked through a patch of dirt with a heavy little hand tool, wishing she could slice through her worries the way she did these troublesome roots.

"That sounds ominous," he said. "Anything you care to talk about?"

Tessa thought about the file folder sitting in her desk drawer. She knew she couldn't talk about that to anyone. Not unless she was ready to be a whistle blower. And she couldn't do something like that when she wasn't even sure if Dunham was doing anything wrong. Like Mr. Morgan had said, there was nothing illegal about using GMOs. She couldn't even be sure if they were dangerous.

"Ever have a moral dilemma?" she asked.

"Once," he said, nodding sagely.

"What about?"

"Well, it was back when I was much more religious."

"You?" Tessa looked him up and down, from his ponytail to his leather sandals. "Religious?"

He laughed while he settled one of his seedlings into a pot. "Believe it or not, Tessa, I was raised to be Very Catholic."

"'Very' Catholic?" Tessa mulled that

over. "As opposed to only 'Slightly' Catholic?"

"Indeed." He winked at her. "The difference is, someone who is only Slightly Catholic only goes to church on holidays, and they celebrate Christmas and Easter more for the presents and candy than for the religious aspects. But my parents wanted me to be Very Catholic, which meant church every Sunday, and always wearing our Sunday best."

"I'm trying to picture you in a suit and tie," Tessa said, smirking. "Nah. Ain't happening."

He chuckled. "Oh, I'll show you some old family photographs sometime. I even had a sensible haircut." He brushed a stray strand of hair back over his shoulder.

"So what happened?"

"Well," he said, pausing in his work and looking off into the distance, "I got into a debate with one of my Very

Catholic friends about something that I couldn't resolve. It came down to a question of morals, and where morals come from."

"Where they come from?" Tessa frowned as she thought that over, while she continued digging through roots in the dirt. "I don't understand."

"Well, here's the way to look at it. Say I gave you a gun."

"You hate guns."

"I know." He laughed. "But hypothetically, say I gave you a gun, walked you into a room, and asked you to shoot a total stranger. Would you do it?"

"Of course not." She frowned at him, not having any idea where this was going.

"Few people would. And that's the key. We could ask anyone here," he gestured with his little shovel to the other gardeners in their plots, "and they'd all say the same thing. They wouldn't shoot the person. No one would, not even Topher."

Tessa glanced across the field at Topher. He was busy digging up dirt with a hoe, talking rather animatedly to himself as he did so. He had to be the most energetic and animated person Tessa knew. Sometimes he gave her the willies.

"Because none of us are psychopaths," Tessa said. *Not even Topher.*

"But then, how do you know you have free will?"

Tessa paused in her work with her rake still dug into the dirt. "I...wow. Okay. Well, I guess I know I have free will because I *could* decide to shoot the person, even though I never would."

"So then what's stopping you?"

Tessa struggled with that for a long moment, but she had no answer.

"My friend," Samson said, "claimed the only thing stopping you is God."

"Hmm." Tessa stood up and stretched

out her back. "I mean, I guess in a way that makes sense. But I don't think I'm Very Religious enough to quite buy that."

"Neither was I." Samson shrugged, then resumed setting his new seedlings into the clay pots. "It seemed to clash so much with my idea of what God was, what free will is meant to be. I couldn't accept the idea that God was like a giant hand, holding me back from doing something bad. And I started thinking about the difference between right and wrong, and how I knew what was right and what wasn't."

He paused with his little shovel stuck in the dirt, a distant look in his eyes. "I realized that the only way I knew how to tell what was right was to look at the bible for answers. And then I realized that so many people over the course of time have looked at those words, and found completely different answers. And many more who claim to follow God don't even follow His word."

He shrugged and went back to his work. "That's when I lost my faith in religion. Not in God, but in organized religion. In the institution of it. And I started looking within myself to find my morals. Analyzing situations to search for the right and wrong within my own heart."

"So what you're telling me is," Tessa said, sighing, "I've got to settle my moral dilemma on my own?"

"Well, I can offer my viewpoint, if you want to talk about it. But you," he pointed the shovel at her, "have to determine your own moral compass. One person's right can easily be another person's wrong."

Tessa pulled off her gloves and grabbed her water bottle. She thought over Samson's words while she took a drink. What was her personal right or wrong? On the one hand, she thought it would be wrong to hide potentially dangerous secrets from the public, if it meant people could get sick. On the other hand, she also knew it would be wrong to risk damaging the company and risking a lot of people's jobs, based on nothing more than a hunch. If word got out that Dunham was using GMOs, it could crush the company's sales, and lead to thousands of layoffs. She didn't want that on her conscience. But she also didn't want the burden of knowing she let people get sick.

"No offense, Samson," she said, "but I think you just made this more complicated for me."

"This is what I do," he said, smiling.

Tessa sighed and pulled her gloves back on. She knelt back down and got back to work, determined not to think about anything complicated for the rest of the day.

Chapter Three

Over the weekend, Tessa did some online research. Most of what she learned wasn't too disheartening. A lot of the studies she read indicated that GMOs weren't necessarily harmful to people. A lot of the benefits even sounded good on the surface: they were easier to grow, resistant to rot and decay, and could provide better vitamins. It almost sounded to Tessa like they were healthier and more beneficial, and for a time she thought that maybe all of the hype around them was nothing more than politics.

But she came across a few studies that were more disturbing. Studies that indicated some types of GMOs could harm the heart, kidney, and liver. And there was another issue that bothered her more. Tessa was a strong supporter of fully organic foods. She never used chemical fertilizers or weed killers. But she learned that there were some types of genetically modified corn that were resistant to chemical weed killers. With normal corn, farmers would need to spray the weed killers only on the weeds, since the chemicals could harm the growth of the corn as well. But these genetically modified "super corns" could take a dose of chemical spray and keep growing just fine. It made things easier on farmers, since they could just douse entire fields with pesticides without worry. Which meant some people were eating corn that had been doused in chemicals. And while the corn might be resistant to it, that didn't mean that people were.

She sat at her computer late Saturday night, her head resting in her hand, a glass of wine sitting by her side. It was a lot more information than she could process. She simply wasn't a scientist. She'd gone to college for a degree in philosophy, and since there were very few job opportunities for philosophers nowadays, she'd taken the best office job she could find. She was starting to wonder whether she'd chosen the right career path.

She refilled her wine glass and walked over to the window, looking out over the darkened garden plots. She tried to imagine what it would be like, growing foods there that had been affected the same way some of the Dunham crops had. She knew that deep down a lot of the fear surrounding GMOs was nothing more than propaganda and politics, which had caused a lot of misunderstanding by the populace. But then she thought about her garden being doused in heavy sprays of toxic chemicals, chemicals that were used more heavily on some GMO crops than on natural crops. She thought about eating fruits and vegetables that had been covered in those chemical sprays, having all of that inside of her, affecting her in she knew not what way.

She shuddered and took a long drink from her wine glass. Maybe it was just her personal superstitions, but she couldn't embrace the idea of eating such things. And as far as she was concerned, a company like Dunham at the very least had a responsibility for transparency. If there was even the smallest danger from their products, then their customers deserved to know the truth. That way, the consumers could make up their own minds. People who supported and endorsed GMOs could be free to eat them, while people like Tessa and her neighbors could stick with their homegrown, fully organic foods.

While she was thinking about all of this, Tessa caught sight of a shadow moving among the fields. She leaned closer to the window, peering outside. It was probably just one of her neighbors, checking their plot. When she focused on the movement, she realized which garden plot the person was working on. It was the one she and Samson had dubbed "The Mystery Plot."

Tessa was on a first name basis with most of her neighbors. They all shared what they grew, and they all helped each other out. But there was one plot, just one, that no one in the community ever worked on. Yet it always thrived. There were magnificent squash, zucchini, and tomatoes there throughout the season, and in the fall there were plump pumpkins growing just in time for Halloween. The rows of crops were always perfectly tilled, the weeds were always pulled, and the produce was harvested at its peak freshness. But no one seemed to know who was doing it.

For awhile, Tessa had assumed that whoever worked on the Mystery Plot tended their crops during the weekdays when a lot of the gardeners were at work. But Samson, who worked nights and weekends at a little music store downtown, said he'd never seen anyone there during the day. A few of the neighbors claimed it must have been a ghost, though Tessa didn't believe in such things.

She set down her wine glass and grabbed a flashlight, then headed out into the garden patch. She walked along the lines of crops without turning the flashlight on until she was at the edge of the Mystery Plot. When she flicked on the light and cast it about the area, she saw nothing but carefully tilled rows of soil. This early in the season, nothing much had grown yet, but someone had started prepping the soil, just as Tessa had in her own plot earlier that day.

She flicked off the flashlight and headed back to her apartment. She had enough worries in her life right now without chasing gardening ghosts. She finished off her wine, turned off the lights, and headed to bed, hoping that a fresh perspective after a good night's sleep would help her get past her moral dilemmas.

TESSA'S SPRING

Chapter Four

At work on Monday, Tessa started doing a little digging. In between meeting her quota for entering files into the computer, she ran some searches through the database of older files. She had a few pages from the file she'd stolen, and she picked out a few keywords from it to search for. She ran searches on the terms "GMO," "pesticides," "safety," "inspection," and a few others. What she found started making her realize there was more to this problem than she'd ever imagined.

She found dozens of files similar to the one she'd first discovered. Hundreds. Many of them dated back years and years, since before she started working at Dunham. After going over a good number of them, she started noticing a pattern. Each report started off with some small, seemingly innocuous problem that one of the inspectors had found. Trace amounts of an unauthorized chemical. Improper labeling of shipments. The discovery of substances that, while not necessarily illegal or dangerous, were certainly not anything that Dunham admitted were being used. And at the bottom of almost every one of these reports, there was a note from the inspector suggesting further investigation. But as far as she could tell, there had never been any further investigation. At least, not in any of the reports that her department processed.

She sat at her computer, drumming her fingers on her desk, wondering what she should do. There was still nothing in these reports to prove that illegal or dangerous chemicals were being used. But there was the possibility. A possibility that seemed pretty likely, given the large number of reports that had gone unchecked. Someone at Dunham Enterprises was either keeping themselves willfully ignorant of the possible risk, or else actively covering it up.

"Whatcha doing?"

Tessa jumped, her hand going to her chest. She looked up to see Mindy's spiky red head sticking up over the wall between their cubicles.

"Geez, jumpy much?" Mindy asked.

"You just startled me." Tessa took a few deep breaths to calm herself. She clicked the button to minimize the report on her screen. "What's up?"

"I was asking you that, Tessy girl." Mindy leaned her arms on the wall and propped her chin on her hands. "You're slacking off today." She nodded to Tessa's outbox, which barely had any files in it. "You never slack off. What's up?"

"It's nothing." Tessa grabbed another file from her inbox and opened it. "I just had a long weekend. I'll catch up."

"There's no rush," Mindy said, snorting. She nodded to the several year's worth of backlogged files stacked up against the far wall. "It's not like those are going anywhere."

Tessa glanced over at the stacks of unprocessed files. The most recent files she had entered into the system were from inspections that had taken place over three years ago. Most of the ones she'd found in the database were even older. If there had been any followup, she realized, then the files would still be in the boxes of backlogged reports. That was where she had to look.

After Mindy went back to work, Tessa headed over to the stacks of boxes. She didn't know where to begin. All of the boxes were dated, marking when they'd received the reports. But they received reports from hundreds of branches across the country.

She checked the file number on the first report she'd taken. Some of the reports they processed, such as the inventory reports, were compiled monthly. But a lot of the safety inspections were only conducted twice a year. She headed down the line of boxes until she found some from six months ago, then dug through them until she found a file with a matching number to the one she already had. She searched again until she found another report from a year ago, a year and a half ago, two years ago, and so on, until she had a stack of consecutive reports from the same facility.

She brought the reports back to her desk and started looking through them, starting with the oldest one. It was written by the same inspector who'd filled out the first report, and it contained more notes at the bottom urging for a more detailed inspection of the facility. But the next report was written by someone else entirely. There was no way for her to know if the first inspector had quit, gotten fired, or simply been transferred to a different location. But the next inspector, for whatever the reason, reported that nothing was out of the ordinary at all.

There was a similar pattern throughout the reports. Here and there, she found reports that indicated a possible problem, only to find that the inspector who had reported it was no longer working at the same facility by the following year. And the new inspector never found any problems at first. It could have been because they were intentionally covering things up. Or because they simply didn't know what to look for without having seen the previous inspector's reports. But whatever the reason, there were three years of reports, six files in all, but no inspector had remained at the same location for more than a year.

She took out some key pages from several of the reports and photocopied them, then returned the files to the boxes where she'd found them. She made note of the name on the most recent report, which had been filed only a month ago. It was written by a woman named Elizabeth O'Conner.

She searched through the company's HR database until she found a phone number and extension for Mrs. O'Conner, at Dunham's Eastern Pennsylvania branch. It was time for Tessa to find out what was really going on here.

Chapter Five

"Hello, Elizabeth O'Conner speaking, how may I help you?"

"Hi," Tessa said. She stood in her apartment, pacing around her living room. She'd gotten off work early so she could go home and make the phone call before O'Conner left her own office. "My name is Tessa Cunningham, and I'm with the Dunham Department of Information Resources. I've just gone over your most recent inspection report."

"Oh," the woman said. Her voice sounded tense. "I wasn't expecting a response so soon. Is something wrong?"

"Well," Tessa said, "that's kind of what I'm calling to find out. You see, we sometimes need to follow up on reports that indicate any possible problems, and you had a few notes in your report that raised some red flags."

Technically, this was only half-true. It was part of Tessa's job to investigate the reports and ensure they were accurate. But she was supposed to report any serious problems to Mr. Morgan. She already knew that he wouldn't look into this any further. She just hoped he didn't find out that she'd been taking matters into her own hands.

"Is this about the pesticide tests?" Elizabeth asked. "I made note of them in my report. There was nothing that went above the minimum safety levels, but..."

"But?" Tessa stood still, holding the phone in a tight grip.

"Well..." Elizabeth hesitated, and Tessa could almost hear the woman mulling it over in her head. "I'm not sure what exactly it is you want from me. I filed my report, and I made sure everything was done according to protocol."

"That's true. But you also noted in your report that you think there might be a need for further investigation."

"Are you investigating me?"

"What?" Tessa asked. "No...no. It's not that. You're not in any trouble or anything."

"Then what's going on?" Elizabeth asked. "I've worked at four different facilities and done plenty of inspections. No one's ever called me to follow up on one."

"I'm just trying to find out if there's some kind of risk."

"I can't say."

"Can't?" Tessa asked. She frowned. "What does that mean."

There was a long pause. Tessa waited for awhile, then checked her phone screen to see if the call was still connected. "Hello?" Tessa asked.

"I'm here." There was another long pause. "Look, I don't want to stir up any trouble, you understand?"

"I understand." Tessa nervously smoothed the front of her shirt. "I don't want that, either. I just want to find out if there's anything going on that we should be concerned with."

"Are you authorized to order a more detailed study?" Elizabeth asked. "My facilities here are a bit limited. We only have the equipment to run basic tests, checking for harmful levels of any chemicals and pesticides, that sort of thing. We green-light shipments, and they go out. To run more detailed tests, you'd need to have things sent off to an independent lab."

Tessa chewed on her lip. She didn't have the first clue how to go about that sort of thing. She racked her brain, trying to figure out what she should do.

"Can you authorize something like that?" Elizabeth asked.

"No. Not exactly."

"What, exactly? Who are you,

J.L. STARR   39

anyway? What's your position?"

"I'm a data entry clerk," Tessa said.

Elizabeth muttered a curse. "Damn, I don't believe this. I thought you were management. I shouldn't even be talking to you."

"Wait, but—"

Elizabeth hung up before Tessa could get another word in. Tessa stood there, staring at the phone. She'd given her name and department to the woman. If Elizabeth decided to report this...

Tessa set her phone down and rubbed her face with both hands. She was too pent up, her muscles tense, her thoughts running a mile a minute. She imagined Elizabeth reporting her to Mr. Morgan, or someone else in the company. She wondered if they'd fire her, or if she could get into legal trouble for overstepping her bounds. Even if she hadn't technically done anything that was against company policy, there was a chance she'd be terminated just because she knew too much. Except that she didn't really know anything. Not yet.

All she knew was that Dunham was using crops that were supposedly resistant to pesticides, and as a result, they were using some kind of pesticide that had alarmed several inspectors enough for them to report it. What if, she thought, those pesticides were being used at dangerous levels? What if their products were making people sick, and no one knew about it?

She considered what Elizabeth O'Conner had said. Most of Dunham's inspections, the ones that went through Tessa's department, at least, were conducted internally. And it would be an easy thing for the company to set up procedures that would keep their own inspectors from finding anything dangerous. They might not even know what to look for. Or, like Elizabeth had said, they might not possess the right equipment needed to find what they were looking for.

The only way she could think to find out would be to get an external lab involved.

That, she knew, would mean crossing a line that she couldn't come back from.

Chapter Six

A few days passed. Tessa was out working in her garden one sunny afternoon. She still hadn't figured out what, if anything, she was going to do. Part of her still wanted to drop the whole issue. It wasn't like she had proof that Dunham was making people sick. There was just the small possibility.

A possibility no one else at the company was investigating.

She pulled out a few handfuls of weeds and old roots, dropping them into a big plastic bucket. Then she carried the bucket to one of her neighbor's plots. Mrs. Mackenzie was an elderly widow with arthritis, so Tessa helped her out a lot with carrying out her garbage or sometimes bringing in groceries. She knelt down at a pile of leaves and weeds that Mrs. Mackenzie had raked out of her own plot, and dropped them into the bucket. The wet leaves weighed more than she'd expected, weighing the bucket down. Tessa grasped the heavy bucket by the handle and headed off to the compost bin.

Her strength started to give out just when she got to the bin. She set the bucket down for a moment, took a deep breath, then hauled the bucket up to dump it into the compost bin.

It slipped out of her grasp, spilling leaves, roots, weeds, and specks of dirt all over the ground.

"Darn it," she muttered. She was almost tempted to leave it all there. It wasn't like it was real litter when it was all biodegradable plant matter. But her neighbors would get irritable with her about it, and she didn't want to do something like that just because she was lazy.

She knelt down and started scooping up the debris, hauling it into the bin a double-handful at a time. When she was grabbing her second handful, someone crouched down next to her and started lending a hand.

"Had a little accident?"

She looked up and saw it was Mr. Jones. He was an elderly African American man who lived in Tessa's building. She didn't see him out and about much, other than when he was checking the mail or taking out his trash. There were rumors that he was an ex-con, and some people claimed he'd spent several decades in jail for a murder committed when he was a young man. Tessa couldn't see that in him. Even though they didn't talk much, he was always so reserved.

"This is what I get for not making two trips," Tessa said, scooping up some more leaves.

"No harm done," Mr. Jones said. He

smiled at her, revealing the deep lines in his face. There was a sadness to his smile. As if he knew he only had so many smiles to give, and each one was the loss of something beautiful.

Working together, they cleaned up the mess in no time. "Thanks," she said, brushing off her hands. "Have a nice day."

"You do the same."

He watched her walk away as she circled around the building. He watched people a lot, she noticed. His apartment had one of the best views of the garden plot, and on many days he sat at his rear window, sipping tea, and watching the community around him as they worked on making things grow.

Tessa paused in her step, thinking it sad that such a sweet old man could only ever watch the making of life. She wondered if he would ever be interested in a patch of his own. She turned to ask him if he'd ever considered it, but he was already gone.

When she got back to her garden plot, Tessa found Samson there. He had a thermos and a few cups in his hand, and he was pouring some tea for a few of the neighbors. He poured her a cup and handed it to her. "For one of the loveliest gardeners in the community," he said. "After Mrs. Mackenzie, of course." He winked at her.

"Oh, stop," Mrs. Mackenzie said, waving a hand at him and chuckling. "I could be your grandmother."

Mrs. Mackenzie took her tea back to her own plot. Tessa stood with Samson, sharing a drink with him. He looked at her over the rim of his cup, studying her. "You're just a little ball of overwhelming stress today, aren't you?"

Tessa's shoulders slumped. "Is it that obvious?" She still hadn't told anyone about her situation at work. The burden of it was starting to get to her.

"Only because I'm used to seeing you

so chipper."

"Me?" she asked. "Chipper?" She gave him a look of mock irritation and rolled her eyes. "Please. I'm Grumpy McGrumpypants all the time. I'm really starting to hate my job."

"Then quit."

"Ha!" Tessa snorted and shook her head. "Yeah, sure. Just quit."

"Why not?"

Tessa planted a fist on her hip and tilted her head to the side, raising her eyebrows at him. "Umm, hello? Rent, groceries, cell phone bill, et cetera."

Samson shrugged. "Get a different job. One without all the stress. I can talk to the boss down at the music shop."

Tessa shook her head. "Thanks, but I'll manage." She had left the retail world after she finished college. That sort of career might be right for Samson, but he was clearly the sort of person who didn't have any aspirations of promotion and advancement. He would probably be content to work at the same little music shop for the rest of his life. Tessa couldn't imagine dealing with that. She'd hated working in retail. Customers could be so demanding.

"Well," Samson said, pausing to sip his tea, "if there's anything I can do, you just let me know."

Tessa sighed and shook her head. "Not unless you know any chemists or biologists."

"Sure," Samson said. "My friend Gregory, he works at the university. Part time professor, full time researcher. What do you need a chemist for?" He frowned at her in puzzlement.

Tessa blinked, staring at Samson for a moment. "Wait, you really know a chemist?" She downed the rest of her tea, then set the mug down on one of Samson's benches. "Can he like, run tests? For things like chemical fertilizer?"

Samson's eyes narrowed slightly.

"This isn't about Topher, is it?"

They both glanced down the line of gardens at one of their more irritable neighbors. Topher was always overly-energetic, he who talked too much, and he never seemed to understand when Tessa was trying to avoid him. He grew vegetables that he took down to gardening shows, where he could win prizes for the biggest zucchini or the most perfectly shaped tomato. His crops were always bigger and thrived more than anyone else's. Tessa was pretty sure he used some kind of chemical fertilizer, despite the community rule that everything had to be natural and organic.

She shook her head. "No, it's not about him. But...if I brought your friend some samples, do you think he could run some tests for me?"

"Sure, I could ask. He'd want to know what it was for..." There was a look in Samson's eyes that told Tessa he was curious what this was about himself.

"I'll explain later. I've...got some things to figure out."

She gave him a quick hug, then gathered her gardening supplies and headed back into her apartment. She quickly washed up, then turned on her computer and logged onto the Dunham network. She searched through it until she found the forms she was looking for, then printed them out.

She sat in her living room with the pages in hand, tapping her fingers against them. What she was considering could get her fired. But this issue wouldn't stop bugging her. She simply had to know.

And if she was going to pull it off, she realized, she was going to need help.

Chapter Seven

Tessa paced around Samson's apartment, wringing her hands. He'd offered her some tea, though what she really needed was a stiff drink. "I want you do understand," she said, "I'm not sure what I'm asking you to do is strictly legal."

"Is it important?" he asked. Samson sat on a wicker chair, watching her pace. The entire apartment was decorated in wicker, rattan, throw rugs, and oriental lamps. There was an odd yet appropriate clashing to the decor. Nothing about it quite fit together, just like sometimes Tessa couldn't quite fit the things she knew about Samson together.

"I think it is," she said. "It could be nothing. Nothing but covering up harmless use of GMOs because they're afraid of the bad publicity."

"But?"

"But," Tessa said, "it could be something more. I've seen a lot of reports indicating possible harmful levels of pesticides. Which could be hurting people. And the only way to find out is to get some tests done."

"Okay," Samson said. He slapped his hands on his knees and nodded, a determined look on his face. "What is it you need me to do?"

"Help me sneak samples out of one of our main sorting facilities."

He frowned and rubbed his chin. "Can't we just get some Dunham products from the supermarket?"

"No." Tessa made a cutting gesture with her hands. "That won't be good enough. Dunham's produce is triple-washed before it goes to the markets. In theory that helps make it safe, but residue from pesticides can be absorbed by the produce, or stick to the skin. Especially the skins of certain fruits, like apples. I think we need to get some samples before they've been washed, so we can get a complete sample. Find out exactly what's going into this food. Even if it's only in there at reduced levels after the produce has been washed, it might be the sort of thing that becomes dangerous when consumed in large quantities over a long period of time."

"And you're worried those 'reduced levels' will be low enough to slip past most tests," Samson said, "but high enough to still be dangerous."

"I think so." Tessa threw up her arms. "I mean, I don't know. I'm not a scientist. I'm going off what I've learned from online research here. But I have a list of some of the highest-risk fruits and vegetables. Apples, strawberries, grapes, celery, peaches. A few others. I want to get samples of each."

"Okay." Samson stood up and walked

over to her, sticking his hands in his pockets. "So, you work for them. You can get us in, right?"

Her face scrunched up. "Sort of?"

"Uh-oh." He rubbed his chin. "What does 'sort of' mean?"

"It means I found copies of all the forms needed to get the goods released to us, but I'm technically not authorized to submit the orders. I'd need signatures from upper management, like my boss, Mr. Morgan. And that's not going to happen."

"So, if I'm hearing you right," Samson said, smiling, "you need someone to play the role of 'Mr. Morgan' during your visit to the sorting facility."

Tessa shrugged, her lips twisting in a wry grin. "Do you own a suit?"

* * *

They pulled up to the Dunham Enterprises Eastern Pennsylvania

Sorting Facility mid-Saturday morning, driving a rented pickup truck. Tessa was dressed in her smartest business suit, with a cream-colored blouse and maroon pants and jacket. This wasn't an unusual look for her; she dressed like this whenever there was an important meeting at work, always conscious of making the best impression.

Samson, on the other hand, was completely transformed. Not only was he wearing a suit and tie, he had also cut his hair. Instead of hanging down to the middle of his back, it was in a short ponytail that just brushed his neck. He was also clean-shaven, and Tessa was pretty sure she detected a hint of cologne.

"You look like a secret agent," Tessa said as they got out of the car.

Samson pulled out a pair of dark sunglasses, put them on, and said, "Just call me Bond. Samson Bond."

They walked up to the facility. Tessa

tried to keep a purposeful stride in her step. People wouldn't be as likely to question them if they looked like they belonged here, like they knew what they were doing.

They walked in the front door and found a bored receptionist sitting at her desk, playing Angry Birds on her computer. Tessa walked right up to the desk and cleared her throat. The receptionist cleared her throat and sat up straight. "Can I help you?" she asked.

"Yes," Tessa said, pulling some papers out of her briefcase and handing them to the girl. "I'm Ms. Cunningham, this is Mr. Morgan. We're from the Department of Information Resources. We're here to pick up some samples for inspection."

The girl looked at the forms, her face tense. She skimmed the pages, licking her lips, but it was clear she had no idea what to do in this situation. "Umm, okay. Do you need me to call the floor manager?"

Tessa almost told the girl no, but she didn't want to raise suspicions. If they were going to make this work, they would need the cooperation of the staff here. "Yes, please," she said. "As long as he's not busy."

"Just one moment." The receptionist picked up her phone and pressed a button. A moment later she told whoever answered about the visitors, then she hung up and said, "It'll be just a moment."

They didn't have to wait long before the manager, a middle-aged man with his shirt sleeves rolled up and his tie hanging loose around his neck, came into the lobby. "Hi," he said, extending a hand first to Samson, then to Tessa. "Mike Carter, assistant floor manager. What's this all about?"

Samson stepped forward, showing Mike a copy of the inspection report from Elizabeth O'Conner. "One of your inspectors filed a report with our department, suggesting the need for more testing on some of the products. We'd like to take a few samples so they can be analyzed. Make sure everything meets with safety specs."

Mike scanned the report, nodding. "All right. Yeah, I remembered her saying something about it. I didn't know there would be anyone coming down here, though."

Samson leaned closer and lowered his voice. "Well, they're trying to keep this quiet. You understand, right? The media hears the words 'health hazard,' and the next thing you know, they've got OSHA and the USDA down our throats, people stop buying our products, and we get the damn hippie health nuts picketing us. Nobody wants that."

Mike nodded, breaking out into a light sweat. "Right. I understand. Though I can assure you, everything at this facility is run according to spec."

J.L. STARR

Samson smiled at the man and patted him on his arm. "Trust me, I know. No one blames you. This is just a sorting facility, after all. You're not responsible for what happens out in the fields."

"That's right," Mike said, a determined set to his jaw. "We just load everything up and send it off to the local distributors in each region."

"Which is why we want to get samples right from the source," Tessa said. "So we can run tests on the produce before it's even been handled by your people. That will prove that any contamination came before any of it even crossed your hands."

Mike blanched at the word "contamination." "Right. Right. Well, just let me know what I can do for you. We'll be happy to help."

They left some paperwork with the receptionist for filing. By the time Mike led them onto the main floor, the girl was already tucking the papers into a filing cabinet, where Tessa hoped they'd be lost and forgotten.

The main part of the facility was a broad, high-ceilinged room, filled with machinery. Crates of produce were unloaded from trucks at the far end of the room, then piled onto conveyor belts. The belts ran them through sprinkler systems that washed and sanitized everything, taking the produce through a triple-wash system to maximize sanitation. The produce was then loaded back into crates and sorted, with the workers loading up shipments that would be taken off to Delaware, New Jersey, New York, and Connecticut. After arriving at their destinations, Tessa knew the shipments would be split up into smaller orders for delivery to supermarkets local to each area.

Mike walked them through the facility, explaining some of the processes. "Everything meets all health code regulations," he said. "Everyone wears gloves and hair nets, and we do a full scrub down of the machinery after every shift."

"Everything looks good," Tessa said. She looked around the room at all of the weekend workers, busy loading and unloading crates and operating the machinery. There were a lot of people here who might recognize her face if someone from Dunham started poking around, trying to find out what she'd done here. She suddenly wished she hadn't used her real name.

"Do you have anything that hasn't been washed yet?" Samson asked. "It'd be best if we got samples right off the truck."

"Sure thing." Mike led them to the loading docks, where several trucks were in the process of being unloaded. "How much do you need, exactly?"

"Just a few pieces from each," Tessa said. "Preferably stuff that was grown in different fields. If there's anything wrong, we want to isolate where it came from."

Mike had some of his people help them with selecting some fruits and vegetables from a variety of crates. Tessa made sure everything got labeled, and she took notes on where each shipment had come from. With the tracking numbers on the crates, she could search the Dunham computer network and find out the exact field these crops had been grown in.

They got some of Mike's men to carry the boxes of samples to the truck. They shook hands again, and before they left, Samson leaned closed and spoke quietly to the man. "Remember, it'd be best if you keep this as quiet as possible. We don't want to risk any bad publicity when there's a good chance this is all just a pointless scare, right?"

"Right," Mike said, nodding. He licked his lips. "Look, my name isn't going to be associated with anything, right? I mean, I just work here."

"Don't worry," Samson said. "We won't even mention you."

Mike wiped the sweat from his forehead and he headed back to the facility. Tessa and Samson got into the truck and drove off. Tessa held her breath until they were out of sight of the facility, then she let out a long sigh of relief.

"That went well," Samson said.

"I hope so." Tessa turned in her seat and looked back behind them, half-expecting someone to be following them. "I just hope no one starts asking any questions or following up on what we just did. This could really bite me in the ass."

She consoled herself with the reminder that this could be for a good cause. If she got fired, but stopped people from getting sick in the process, then it would all be worth it.

Chapter Eight

Tessa and Samson stopped at a gas station a few miles from the shipping facility. While Samson filled the tank, Tessa paced back and forth across the asphalt, fidgeting nervously with her hands. "Wow," she said. "Wow wow wow. I can't believe we just did that."

"It sure was a trip," Samson said. He took off his suit jacket and tie, tossing them into the truck, then rolled up his shirtsleeves. He almost looked like his normal self again, though the gray silk pants were still quite out of character.

"I thought for sure we were going to get caught." Tessa ran her fingers through her hair, feeling pent up with too much energy. "Every time he asked a question, I thought, 'This is it. We're screwed.'"

"It didn't show. You played it totally cool."

"Really?" Tessa smiled bashfully, her face warming up. "I was just trying to keep him from being able to think too much about what was going on. I loved the way you kept pushing him about the risk of the media finding out. Keeping him too nervous to think things through."

Samson leaned against the truck and stuck his hands in his pockets. "All in a day's work for Bond. Samson Bond."

Tessa laughed and stepped forward, throwing her arms around him. "Oh, thank goodness you were here. Thank you for doing this. I can't imagine why you agreed to it. We could have been arrested."

"Well," he said, pulling his hands out of his pockets and slipping them around her waist. "I guess I just couldn't say no to you."

She leaned back and looked into his eyes. There was something there. Something unexpected. Her mouth suddenly felt dry. She'd never really looked at Samson like this before. He was just her hippie neighbor, the man who grew herbs in his garden and made tea for his neighbors. Though he was looking rather handsome, now that he'd cleaned up a little.

The gas pump clicked off with a loud snap, jarring Tessa from her thoughts and making her jump back. She laughed nervously and brushed her hair back just to give her hands something to do. "Well, we should get going," she said. "I'd like to get this stuff to your professor friend right away."

Samson topped off the tank, then they got back in the truck and drove off. Most of the drive was quiet. Tessa kept glancing over at Samson, wondering. She chewed on her lip, trying to sort through her thoughts, but they were all jumbled.

They arrived at the university in mid-afternoon. The campus was mostly empty, with no classes in session on Saturday, though there were some students mingling about here and there. They parked near the science building and Samson led Tessa in to meet his friend. The professor was a young man who fit the image of his job perfectly, from his nerdy glasses to the tan suspenders holding up his pants. Samson made the introductions, introducing his friend as Gregory Harcourt.

"So, what kind of samples is it you want me to look at?" Gregory asked after the introductions.

"We tried to get a little of everything," Tessa said. "I wasn't really sure what would be best. But it's all labeled, based on where it came from."

"Let's take a look," Gregory said.

They hauled the boxes of produce up

to Gregory's office, then started sorting through everything while Gregory took notes on the invoice numbers Tessa had recorded for each sample. "This is a lot of stuff," Gregory said, looking over all the samples. "I'm going to need a few days for all this."

"All right," Tessa said. "Whatever you need. And...thank you. For doing this. I wish we could do something for you..."

Gregory gave her and encouraging smile. "It's all right. Samson explained the situation to me. I guess I consider this my civic duty as a scientist."

He walked them to the door and shook their hands. "I'll let you know as soon as I get the results," he said. "Just keep in mind, all of this will have to be off the record. I can't go on record with any study that hasn't been cleared by the university's Institutional Review Board. If it turns out there's something there, you'll need to report it to the USDA and get them to conduct an official investigation."

"I want to at least find out if there's anything worth reporting first," Tessa said. "After all, there could be thousands of people's jobs on the line here."

"Don't worry," Gregory said. "I'll keep things hushed on my end."

"Thank you." She gave him a grateful smile.

When Tessa and Samson got back to their apartment complex, Samson invited Tessa over for a drink. "After the day we've had," he said, "I think we both deserve a chance to unwind and relax."

"Sounds perfect."

She stopped at her own apartment to change out of her fancy suit and into sweatpants and a tank top, then headed over to Samson's. When she got there, he was in the middle of getting changed himself. He'd traded the suit pants for a tight pair of jeans, and he was still pulling on a clean t-shirt when he opened the door. She got a brief glimpse of his toned abs, and for the first time she appreciated the kind of physique a man could develop when he rode a bicycle everywhere all the time.

Samson poured them each a glass of white wine, then raised his glass and said, "To a successful heist."

Tessa clinked her glass against his. They sat together on his sofa, drinking wine and trying to unwind. Tessa couldn't quite get settled onto the couch, and kept fidgeting. She felt stiff, her back and shoulders all knotted up with tension. Part of her still kept expecting the police to show up at the door. She wasn't sure if anything they'd done was *technically* illegal. It was possible she'd just get fired instead of arrested. Not that that was much comfort.

"You look tense," Samson said. "Here, let me help."

He moved next to her and she turned her back to him. He set down his wine glass, then started rubbing her shoulders. Tessa closed her eyes and let out a long sigh. The aches in her muscles slowly started to fade away. "You're really good at that," she whispered as Samson's fingers massaged her worries out.

"Professional training," he said. "I spent six months training as a physical therapist before I decided it wasn't for me."

"Well, you're just full of endless surprises."

"All part of my charm," he said.

After Samson worked the kinks out of her back and shoulders, Tessa leaned back against him, sipping her wine. She felt more relaxed and at home than she had in a long time. Samson's fingers kept gently running along her arm, tracing delicate touches across her skin. She let out a soft sound of contentment and nestled against him, almost feeling like she could drift off to sleep. She wasn't sure if it was the wine, the massage, or the aftermath of a day filled with adrenaline, but she was ready to crash right there on her neighbor's couch.

Samson's hand slid down her arm until his fingers glided across the back of her hand, then intertwined with her fingers. She held onto his hand, not wanting to let go. His breath felt warm against her neck.

She suddenly stiffened, sitting up a bit straighter. "Samson?" she whispered.

"Yes?"

"What are we doing?"

He was silent for a long moment, though he didn't let go of her hand. "Sitting on the couch," he said, speaking softly. "Drinking wine. Enjoying each other's company."

"Is that all?"

She twisted around to look into his eyes. He looked at her in a way he never had before. His eyes traced the lines of her face, then strayed down to look at her lips. Tessa licked her lips, wondering what he was thinking in that moment. Wondering what was about to happen.

A sound from outside jarred them out of the moment. They both jumped up, looking towards the window.

"What was that?" Tessa asked.

"Probably nothing," Samson said. He stepped over to the window and pulled the curtain back, peering outside. Night had fallen, and the garden plots were draped in darkness.

They headed outside, looking around the plots. After a minute of searching, they came across a jumble of pots and trellises that someone had dropped by the edge of one of the plots. "This wasn't here this morning," Tessa said.

"Ahh," Samson said. He gestured to the shadow-enshrouded plot. "Of course. The Mystery Plot."

"Darn." Tessa looked around, searching for signs of anyone in the darkness. "We must have just missed our mystery gardener. I swear, one of these days, I'm going to set up a camera and see who comes out here."

Samson chuckled. In the dim moonlight and the gentle illumination coming from the apartment building's windows, he looked quite stunning. Tessa looked up at him, stepping closer.

His hand reached out for hers. Their fingers intertwined.

Samson's other hand reached up and he caressed her cheek. Tessa held her breath.

Then he kissed her, there under the moonlight, beside the mysterious garden, while the cool spring wind blew between the apartment buildings and wrapped them in its embrace.

Chapter Nine

Monday at work, Tessa kept looking over her shoulder. There hadn't yet been any word about her escapade over the weekend, but she was sure that someone was going to find out. She searched through the newest box of paperwork that had been delivered that morning, hoping to intercept any reports that mentioned her and "Mr. Morgan" stopping by the Pennsylvania distribution facility. Of course, there weren't any reports yet. Even if someone mailed one in, it wouldn't be there for a couple of weeks.

When Tessa was getting her third cup of coffee—admitting to herself that her nerves probably didn't need any more caffeine—Mindy walked up to her and asked, "So, did you hear?"

Tessa froze with the coffee pot and her "Gardeners Do It in the Dirt" coffee mug in her hands. "Hear what?"

"About Mr. Morgan?"

Tessa's hands started to shake. "What about him?"

Mindy leaned closer, looking around to make sure no one was listening in on them. "Well, Tracy said that Rebecca told her that someone from Mr. Morgan's office saw him slipping out the door Friday night with Mary from Accounting."

Tessa stared at Mindy for a long moment, then she blinked. The tension fled her body when she realized it was nothing more than the usual office gossip. "Isn't Mary married?"

"Pfft, like that would stop her." Mindy crossed her arms and shook her head. "You know all about her and Carl, right?"

Tessa sighed, closing her eyes and

wishing for strength. "I don't really have the energy to keep up with all the latest rumors. I've got a lot of work to do."

"Fine, Miss Grumpypants," Mindy said. "I just thought you'd be interested."

Tessa gave her friend a patient smile. "I'm not trying to be Miss Grumpypants. I just have a lot going on right now."

"Okay." Mindy looked her over with concern in her eyes. "Well, you let me know if there's anything you need, all right?"

"All right."

Tessa kept her head down the rest of the day, focusing on her work. She entered reports into the computer at a steady pace, making surprisingly good progress and putting a nice dent in the backlog of files. She wondered if being on edge was somehow helping her work faster. She was trying so hard to force herself to stay focused on her work that it seemed she'd found a great rhythm. If only she were this anxious every day.

Near the end of the day, when she was shredding files and getting ready to go home for the day, Mr. Morgan walked into the office. Tessa avoided eye contact, not wanting to draw any attention to herself. But he walked right up to her. "Tessa? Can I see you in my office for a moment."

Tessa silently cursed herself, but kept a stoic expression on her face. "Sure."

She followed him to his office. He shut the door behind them and offered her a seat. Mr. Morgan sat down and folded his hands on the desk, then asked, "Have you talked to anyone about that issue you brought up to me the other day?"

"Me?" Tessa faked a laugh and shook her head. She kept her hands firmly in her lap to keep them from shaking. "No. Why?"

"Because I just got a call from a reporter," he said. "He was asking for information about pesticide use in our products. He claimed he was contacted by an anonymous source who said they worked for us. That this source said something about toxic pesticides in our products."

"Holy moly," Tessa said. She clutched at her skirt until her knuckles turned white. "Oh, gosh, no. I swear to God it wasn't me. I would never call a reporter!"

She wracked her brain, trying to think who might have called in the leak. Could Samson have done it? Would he have leaked the information without telling her?

"Is there anyone else you think might have heard about those reports?" Mr. Morgan asked. Anyone you mentioned it to? Anyone who might have gotten wind of your concerns?"

That's when it clicked. She'd talked to a number of people at the sorting facility in Pennsylvania. The receptionist. Mike the weekend manager. Half a dozen employees who'd helped them load the samples into the truck. Any one of them might have decided to call in the report.

"I have no idea who it could be," she said. "I haven't talked to anyone."

"You're sure?" He studied her expression, and she was sure he'd see the lie.

"I'm sure." She forced herself to meet his gaze, hoping there was nothing in her eyes that betrayed her.

"All right." Mr. Morgan sighed and looked through some notes on his desk. "I need to figure out what kind of statement to give this guy. We can't afford to have the media start a witch hunt. We could all lose our jobs because of someone's unfounded paranoia."

"Unfounded?" she asked. "Are you sure it's unfounded? I mean, those reports..."

"Those reports located a very minor, isolated problem," Mr. Morgan said. "It happens now and then. Someone at one of the farms accidentally mixed together two types of pesticide that weren't supposed to be mixed, and the combination of the two led to a very minor, we're talking less than one percent here, a very minor risk. We corrected the problem, recalled the affected products, and got everything back up and running again. It happens."

"Wait," Tessa said, her mouth going dry. "What? I thought you told me—"

"I told you not to worry about it," Mr. Morgan said. "That didn't mean I was ignoring it. It's not your job to worry about that sort of thing. Your job is to enter the reports into the databases, so that our Quality Assurance department can conduct their investigations. *Internal* investigations, so that we don't have messes like this happening." He gestured to the notes about the reporter and the apparent leak.

"But the things you said..." Tessa

frowned, shaking her head.

"I told you that nothing illegal was going on," Mr. Morgan said. "And nothing is. We comply with USDA inspections and follow all regulations, just like every other business. But for minor things, we take care of it on our own and make sure it stays quiet. That way we avoid bad publicity."

Tessa felt faint. She tasted bile in her throat. Her entire concern, all of the risks she'd taken... "So there really wasn't any risk? Our food isn't contaminated?"

"Of course not." Mr. Morgan frowned at her. "What kind of business do you think we're running here? Sure, in a company this large, there are going to be minor issues now and then. You can't avoid that with hundreds of facilities across the country. But the problems are always fixed, the people responsible are retrained to make sure they don't mess up again, and we go about business as usual."

"I see." Tessa stared at the wall behind Mr. Morgan, seeing her entire career flashing before her eyes.

"Now, if you'll excuse me, Tessa," Mr. Morgan said. "I've got to figure out what kind of statement to give this reporter so he doesn't get the wrong idea. If he writes a story with a headline like 'Dunham Enterprises Denies Pesticide Contamination,' it won't matter what the facts are. People see a denial as proof of guilt, even when there is none."

Tessa got up and left, her steps stiff and wooden. She clutched her purse against her chest, holding onto it like a life preserver. She couldn't believe what she'd just heard.

She may have accidentally set events into motion that could cost thousands of people their jobs. And it looked like it had all been for nothing.

Chapter Ten

As soon as Tessa got home that night, she called up Gregory at the university. When he answered, she said, "Hey, this is Tessa. I need to know about the results of those tests."

"Well, I haven't finished with all of the samples yet," he said. "But I can give you the results from the ones I've tested so far."

"Okay." She paced around her apartment chewing on her lower lip. When she'd first come up with this idea, she'd thought these tests would give her answers that would lend her peace of mind. Now she feared the exact opposite.

"Well, so far, all the samples I've tested have come back negative."

"Negative?" Tessa asked. She paused in her pacing. "Negative sounds bad."

"No, no, negative is good. It means there's nothing there."

Tessa felt her stomach churn. "Nothing?"

"Nothing at all. Well, I've found a few tiny trace amounts, but nothing that you wouldn't expect to find on just about any commercially grown product. Nothing that would be harmful."

"Oh gosh."

There was a long pause, then Gregory asked, "That's a good thing, isn't it? I mean, that's what I think you'd want to hear. No harm done. No one's getting sick from eating this stuff."

"Shoot," Tessa said. "Shoot, shoot, shoot!"

"Umm...is something wrong?"

"I have to go."

Tessa hung up the phone before Gregory could say another word. She sat down on her couch, clutching her phone in her hands. Mr. Morgan had been right. There were no pesticides, no risks. Dunham Enterprises wasn't guilty of anything at all, except for maybe failing to advertise that some of their crops had been genetically modified in a completely harmless way.

"Shoot." She stared at the carpet, unable to think. She was certain she was going to get fired. Not only that, but if the reporter—the reporter who was only snooping around because she'd riled up suspicions at the sorting facility—if he wrote a story about a possible contamination and a cover-up within the company, then a lot of people would lose their jobs. Mr. Morgan had been right about another thing: it wouldn't matter that there was actually no risk. Once consumers got it in their heads that Dunham was covering something up, even if it wasn't true, they'd never trust the company again. Sales would drop, people would get laid off, and thousands of lives would be ruined.

And it was all Tessa's fault.

* * *

"I don't understand," Samson said after she explained the situation to him. "I thought you said you'd seen all those reports? All of the inspectors requesting further investigation, but with no followup?"

Tessa sat on Samson's couch, holding a mug of tea in her hands. He'd spiked the tea with a splash of liquor, and it was starting to help calm her down. "It turns out," she said, "the Quality Assurance department uses a completely different filing system. They collect the reports my department enters into the main databases, then they maintain a separate database for their own reports. I found the file directories for that database, and it's filled with all kinds of reports that show the investigations they've conducted and the actions they undertook to correct the problems."

"But what about the lady you spoke to?" Samson asked. "The one that said no one had followed up on her report. Did you say there were like three years of reports that this QA department had never followed up on?"

Tessa laughed, a wry smile on her face. "Oh, yes. There's three years of reports they never followed up on. Because my department has a three year backlog. Ironic, isn't it? Here I was thinking there was some grand conspiracy to keep things hidden, and it turns out it's just because my department can't keep up with the paperwork. All of the reports that we *have* entered, if there was a request for a followup investigation, they took care of it."

"Oh." Samson chewed on his lower lip, looking down at the ground. "Well. Damn."

"Yup." Tessa sighed. "I'm so sorry I got you involved in all of this. I had no idea what a mess it would turn out to be."

"So, what do we do now?" Samson asked. "Talk to this reporter? Maybe explain to him that we were just chasing a wild goose?"

"I'm not sure that would even help." Tessa threw herself back against the couch cushions. "If we try to convince him there's nothing to hide, he'd just think there's something to hide. And the more we make Dunham look guilty, the more likely it is that people will start losing their jobs."

Samson sat next to her and patted her knee. She leaned her head against his shoulder and closed her eyes. "We'll figure something out," Samson said.

"Are you sure?"

"No," he said. "But it seemed like the thing to say."

Tessa nuzzled against him, trying to

banish her thoughts and her worries, at least for the moment. The only good part about this whole fiasco, she supposed, was that it had brought Samson and her closer together.

* * *

Over the next few days, Tessa tried to stick to her work and mind her own business. She couldn't think of any way to fix the problems she'd caused, so she was determined to do her best not to make anything worse. No more zany schemes, no more deception, and no more trying to poke her nose into things that clearly weren't any of her business.

The one thing she did keep doing was watching out for any new reports that were coming in from the Pennsylvania sorting facility. It would be easy to intercept them, since no one tended to look at new reports the day they came in. It was more than a week after her visit to the facility that the report she'd been fearing finally came in.

She brought it over to her desk, along with her normal stack of files awaiting data entry. She flipped through the pages, thinking at first that everything was fine. The report had been filed by Elizabeth O'Conner, the woman Tessa had spoken to on the phone. Everything Elizabeth had recorded looked perfectly normal. There were no notes about contamination, making it seem that Elizabeth's previous concerns had been unfounded. Which Tessa already knew, after the test results she'd gotten back from Gregory.

On the last page of the report, where the investigator listed their personal notes and comments, was where Tessa found something that set off alarms in her head. It was a note about the surprise visit to the facility, along with a complaint that Elizabeth hadn't been notified about the surprise inspection.

At the end, Elizabeth noted a rather personal grievance:

I would like to note that it was both discourteous and unprofessional for Mr. Morgan and his assistant to visit our facility without notifying me, considering how the results of any inspection reflect upon both me and my work. And considering I was the one who requested further investigation to begin with, I believe I deserved to be informed of what was happening. I will be requesting a review of appropriate company procedures through the Quality Assurance department, and filing a formal complaint with Human Resources.

Tessa buried her face against the pages, wishing she could just crawl under the reports and drown.

She was done for. Her career was over. As soon as Elizabeth's grievances were filed, Mr. Morgan would find out that someone had impersonated him during the visit to the Pennsylvania facility. It would be traced back to Tessa, and she'd be fired.

She sat at her desk the rest of the day without doing any of her work. She just didn't see the point.

Chapter Eleven

That night, Tessa knelt in her garden, with her hands shoved into the loose, fertile soil. She'd forgotten to wear her gloves, and the black dirt stained her fingers and got stuck under her nails. She knelt there, unmoving, tears welling in her eyes. She couldn't think, couldn't focus. Even her garden didn't seem to be able to relieve her stress that day.

It was a chilly day, and no one else was in the garden. Though Tessa felt like there was someone watching her. She glanced over her shoulder, seeing no one. Until she looked into one of the apartment windows and saw her elderly neighbor, Mr. Jones, looking out at her. He often sat in his apartment and watched the gardeners, though since she was the only one out there, he was watching only her. There was a sad, sympathetic look in his eyes. Like he knew the pain she was feeling.

He raised a hand to her in a small wave. She pulled her hand from the dirt and waved back.

A few moments later, it started to rain. The water came down in a harsh downpour, soaking her almost instantly. She got up and hurried to her apartment, only to find the back door was locked.

"Damn." She patted her jeans, searching for her keys. Then she remembered. In her emotional daze, she'd forgotten to take them out of her purse, which was sitting inside.

She tried her bedroom window, but of course it was also locked. She had a friend on the other side of town who had a spare key, but of course her cell phone was inside the apartment too, so she couldn't even call for help.

Tessa stood out there in the rain, her shoulder slumped, until her tears started to flow freely. They mixed with the rain on her cheeks, invisible against the storm. She couldn't get her thoughts to clear, and in that moment, nothing really seemed to matter anymore.

Then suddenly, the rain stopped falling on her head. The storm still raged around her, but no longer touched her. She looked up and saw a red umbrella being held over her head. The rain drops splattered against it and slid off, playing out a staccato rhythm in the night.

"Not a good night to be out in the weather."

She turned around and saw Mr. Jones there, holding the umbrella, protecting her from the storm. "Lock yourself out?" he asked.

She nodded, wiping her face on the back of her damp sleeve. "I'm an idiot," she said. "I left my keys inside, and..."

"Come on," he said, taking her hand.

"Let's get you inside and get you dry. You can use my phone if you like."

"Thank you." She let him lead her into his apartment, which was warm and cozy after the cold rain. The furniture was old and worn, most of it looking like mismatched pieces bought from yard sales or the Goodwill store. The lights were subdued, almost as if Mr. Jones were afraid to see himself in the light. Red cloths covered several of the lamps, giving the apartment the feeling of eternal dusk.

"Here," Mr. Jones said, handing her a towel. "Make yourself at home. It's not often I have company."

"Thank you, Mr. Jones. I really appreciate your help." She wiped her hands on the towel, scrubbing off the rain and the dirt.

"Oh, call me Terry," he said. "We're neighbors, after all."

She gave him a grateful smile, though she didn't feel like she deserved his neighborly aid. She'd never spoken to him much, beyond the occasional chat while getting her mail.

She used Terry's phone to call her friend, then settled in to wait. It would be at least thirty minutes until her friend could get there, particularly with the storm. Terry made a pot of tea and set out a plate of gingersnaps.

"So," Terry said as he settled into the recliner across from her, "you seem like a woman who has some troubles weighing her down."

"Was it that obvious?" she asked with a wry laugh.

He smiled and blew on his tea to cool it off. "Well, after the life I've lived, I know a thing or two about troubles."

Tessa hesitated, then decided to finally ask the question that she'd had on her mind since she first met him. "Is it true you were in jail?"

He nodded, a sad look in his eyes. "Thirty five years. Half of my life,

J.L. STARR

wasted. All because of a stupid mistake."

"Do you mind if I asked what happened?"

He got a distant look in his eyes, as if looking back across the long years. "I had a problem with drugs, back then. But the real problem was how I let that problem affect everything else." He looked her in the eye. "You see, I let myself do a lot of stupid things, all because I couldn't face my real problem. I was arrested for armed robbery, and for accidentally shooting a man when the gun went off. I just thank God the poor fellow wasn't too seriously hurt."

"Oh, wow." Tessa looked down into her tea mug. "I can't imagine."

"Most people can't." He chuckled. "The thing of it was, I know now that if I'd made the right decision, admitted that I had a problem, I could have stopped things from spiraling out of control. I was deluded back then. Didn't want to admit that the drugs had a hold on me. I thought I was in control of them. That I could do whatever I wanted. And I ended up hurting people, and ruining my own life in the process."

Tessa thought about the mistakes she'd made over the past few weeks. They paled in comparison to what Terry was describing, though there was one similarity. She hadn't wanted to admit that she was in over her head. One mistake had led to another, and now the consequences were starting to spiral out of control.

"How do you fix something like that?" she asked. "I mean, once you can see that it's all out of control, how do you stop it? It's not like you can go back and undo the things you've done."

He looked at her, weighing her, and she was sure he knew she was really talking about her own problems. "The answer is a lot simpler than you realize. You just need to come clean. I thought I could cover up my problems. Hide from them. Take matters into my own hands. And I just kept making things worse. But if I'd gone to someone, to my friends, to my parents, and admitted that I had a problem, I could have gotten help."

"But weren't you afraid of the consequences?"

"Sure I was." He laughed, shaking his head. "I was afraid that I'd end up in jail. But guess what? I ended up worse off, with a longer sentence than I would have had for just the drugs. If I'd accepted my mistakes and been ready to face the music, instead of running from it, then yes, I would have suffered the consequences. But running from those consequences made things so much worse in the long run."

Tessa hung her head. She knew that Terry was right. Maybe, she thought, she could minimize the damage if she just came clean. She might still lose her job. But if she could stop the situation from getting any more out of hand, then maybe she could protect the jobs of her coworkers.

"I know it sounds cliche," Terry said, watching her carefully. "But honesty really is the best policy. Lies always catch up to you, in the end."

Tessa set down her tea. She nodded, keeping her eyes lowered. "You're right. You're definitely right."

When her friend arrived, Tessa thanked Terry for the tea, and for the company. "You should come out and join us sometime," she said. "It'd be nice to see you out in the gardens. There's a couple of unclaimed plots, if you want one of your own."

"Oh, I have my little garden," he said, nodding out the window.

Tessa looked outside and followed his gaze. He was looking right at the Mystery Plot. "That...that one's yours?" She laughed, shaking her head. "We could never figure out who it belonged to! It's so beautiful. Why don't I ever see you tending it?"

He shrugged. "After so many years in isolation, I tend to get nervous around crowds. I go out early in the mornings, before the rest of you are up. Or check in on things at night. It's my way."

"Well, if you ever change your mind," Tessa said, "just know you've got a friend out there."

She gave him a hug, then left his apartment, buried deep in thoughts about the things he'd said.

Chapter Twelve

Tessa knocked on Samson's door, rehearsing in her head what she was about to say. He answered wearing only a pair of sweatpants, his bare chest glistening with moisture and his hair damp. He was rubbing a towel along the back of his hair, sopping up the dampness from his pony tail. "Hey there," he said, stepping back to invite her in. "What's up?"

"I think I need to confess." She walked right past him and sat down on his couch, wringing her hands together.

"Okay." He shut the door and came over to join her, sitting on the coffee table and taking her hands in his. When she kept fidgeting, he wrapped his hands gently around hers, holding them until she stopped trembling and settled down.

"What do you think?"

"I think it's your choice," he said. "Do you want me to come with you? I'm a part of this, after all."

"No," she said. "No, the worst they can really do is fire me. You, they could possibly press charges against."

"I'm willing to face that risk if it means supporting you," he said. "I can't just stand aside and let you take all the blame."

"But it was my idea."

"And I helped you with it." He reached up and caressed her cheek.

She closed her eyes and nuzzled her face against his hand. His touch, his support had meant the world to her while she worked through this crazy situation. But she knew she couldn't risk letting any of the consequences from this fall onto him.

"My mind's made up," she said. "This was my idea, it was my mistake. And I'm going to go face the music."

Samson sighed. She looked into his eyes, making sure he knew how serious she was. "All right," he said. "But is there anything I can do?"

Tessa thought about what she was going to have to face. The likelihood of getting fired. The public humiliation. She imagined being paraded before a board of directors and told she had to explain herself. She wasn't sure she would be able to handle that.

"Just hold me," she whispered.

Samson moved onto the couch with her and pulled her close against him. She closed her eyes and laid her head against his chest. He stroked her hair and held her tight. His warmth, the comfort of his touch, made her feel like maybe there was a chance that everything could be okay.

* * *

Tessa walked into the office Monday

morning wearing her best suit, with her hair done up in a chignon knot. She felt more like she was dressed for a job interview than for the meeting that would end in her termination. But, she figured, if she was going to go down, she would go down in style.

She didn't even bother to go to her desk. She'd stop by later to get the few photographs she kept there, and her coffee mug. But to begin with, she would face her fate and do it with her chin held up high.

She walked right into Mr. Morgan's office and found him waiting there behind his desk. He looked up at her. "Ahh, Tessa. I'm glad you're here, I was about to call you in."

She froze mid-step. Why had he been about to call her? Had he already discovered what she was about to confess?

She stepped over to the desk and sat down, her confidence wavering. "Yes?"

she asked.

"There've been some leads in the situation from the Pennsylvania sorting facility."

Her heart hammered in her throat. If he already knew, then confessing wouldn't help her. She'd hoped to take the high ground, with the possibility that maybe her honesty would dampen the consequences. But it seemed like it was too late.

"I wanted to get your take on this," Mr. Morgan said, holding up some papers. "Since you were the one who first brought it to my attention. I'm thinking we might have been set up."

"Set up?" She took the papers and looked them over. She recognized a few of them immediately. They were the falsified forms that she'd had Samson fill out, signing his forged "Jebediah P. Morgan" signature. Some of the other pages were printouts of emails, including some from people claiming to be environmental activists.

"I...I'm afraid I don't understand," Tessa said. "What do these emails have to do with it?"

"The company gets ridiculous things emailed to us all the time." He gestured to the papers. "Most of the time we just sent out form letter responses, unless a complaint has some greater amount of weight. Some of the more preposterous things we get are threats from environmental groups and wacko liberal hippies who claim we're destroying the environment." He snorted and shook his head. "They threaten to sue, or to expose us as frauds, that sort of thing. Our official company policy is not to bother responding to such threats. They're completely baseless, and responding just encourages these people."

"I'm still not following," Tessa said.

"Read this one." He reached across the desk and pulled out one page from the stack. Tessa took it and read it over.

Her throat started to feel tight as she read it.

"This person says they have proof we're selling people contaminated goods," she said, scanning the page. "But...but I thought we knew everything was clean? There's nothing more than harmless trace amounts of any pesticides."

"You know that, and I know that," Mr. Morgan said. "But this nut job obviously doesn't. Probably some college kid with a home chemistry set and no idea how to tell the difference between actual contamination and trace levels that fall within the USDA safety guidelines. I'm betting whoever this guy is, he's the one who snuck into our facility and stole samples of our produce." He tapped his fingers on the pages with the forged signatures. "Because that sure wasn't me. I've never even been to any of the sorting facilities in person."

Tessa flipped through the pages. Her

head was spinning. "So...what are you going to do?"

"Show these to that reporter," Mr. Morgan said. "Make him realize that someone is trying to set us up. He'll know that there's no story here once he sees what a whack job this guy is. I mean, just look at those emails."

Tessa read the emails again. They certainly sounded like they'd been written by someone who was imbalanced. Most of the text was written in all caps, with lots of excessive exclamation marks and plenty of cursing and threats. It didn't sound like anything that someone could ever take seriously.

She could see the scenario playing out in her mind now. Mr. Morgan would show these emails to the reporter. The reporter would realize that his "lead" on the story was probably this same person, someone who looked more like a conspiracy theorist than an actual environmentalist. The story would be dropped when the reporter realized he might be risking his reputation as a journalist. Dunham Enterprises would be safe. And no one would have to lose their jobs.

All Tessa had to do was lie. Say she hadn't been involved. That she agreed with Mr. Morgan's analysis of the situation. She could encourage him to proceed as he planned, and he'd never be any the wiser.

"So what's your take on this?" Mr. Morgan asked. "You've read up on the inspection reports from that facility. And you've read all of our internal reports on the subject. What do you think?"

Tessa opened her mouth, but no sound came out. She cleared her throat and licked her lips. She didn't know what to say. This was her way out. The universe had handed her the perfect scapegoat. All she had to do was say the words.

"Tessa?"

"I have to tender my resignation."

Mr. Morgan stared at her, dumbstruck. "What? Tessa, what are you talking about?"

"I...I'm the one who did it. These documents," she shuffled through the papers in her lap, "I forged them. I snuck into the Pennsylvania facility, and I stole samples to be tested. I...I was wrong. I shouldn't have done it."

"I don't understand. Tessa, what is this? Are you saying you called this reporter?"

"No...no! Not that."

"Those emails?" He pointed to the pages. "Are those from you?"

"No. Of course not."

"Then I don't get it. How are you saying you're involved in this? Why would you steal from the company? What was going through your mind?"

She hung her head, feeling ashamed.

She'd started out with such noble intentions. She'd thought she would be exposing the corruption of an evil corporation. Saving people from harmful contaminants. But really, she'd just been a fool, seeing a conspiracy where there was none. And it had cost her everything.

"I have no excuse," she said. "I'm sorry. I...I'll go clean out my desk."

She got up and headed for the door.

"Tessa," Mr. Morgan said. "Wait."

She stopped, but couldn't turn back to face him.

Mr. Morgan got up, went over and took the papers from Tessa. She hadn't even realized she was still holding them.

"Sit back down," he said.

Numb from head to toe, Tessa went back to the chair and sat. Mr. Morgan sat on the edge of his desk, holding the papers in his lap. "Now, I want you to start at the beginning," he said, "and tell me what happened."

So she confessed the whole thing, from her first suspicions, to the files she'd taken, to the insane plan to take products from the sorting facility to be used for independent testing. When she finished, she sat there, her shoulders hunched over, her hands folded in her lap. She felt drained. Though at the same time, she felt free. The burden of her lies and her secrets had finally been lifted away.

Mr. Morgan sat there, watching her and rubbing his chin. "So," he said, "you really thought I was trying to cover something up?"

"I'm sorry, Mr. Morgan. I didn't mean to accuse you of anything. I just thought..."

"You just thought that Dunham was a big, faceless corporation where people try to get away with things?" He chuckled and walked over to his filing cabinet, then pulled out a folder. He handed it to her.

"What's this?" She opened the folder and started looking through it.

"One of the recent reports from QA. About one of our old inspectors, who used to work at that Pennsylvania facility. Have you ever wondered why we have such a high turnover rate on our inspectors?"

"I thought they were getting fired for digging too deep," she said. "And finding out things the company didn't want them to know."

"They were fired," Mr. Morgan said, "for not digging deep *enough*. Some of them do a good job, and we transfer them to a bigger facility, where their hard work can have the most impact. Other times, though, we have people like that," he gestured to the file in her hands, "who try to cover up failing reports. See, some of the inspectors think that if their facility gets a failing grade, it looks bad on them. They think they'll be held accountable, so they fudge the reports. Make it look as if everything is fine."

Tessa skimmed the pages. She recognized the inspector's name. He was one of the inspectors who'd written some of the reports she'd read at the start of this whole mess. One of the ones who had reported nothing at all wrong. When she first read his reports, she'd assumed he was hiding some kind of contamination in order to protect the company from exposure. But according to the internal investigation, he'd been doing it to protect his own job. And he'd been fired once the company had found out what he'd done.

"You see, Tessa," Mr. Morgan said, stepping behind his desk and sitting down, "there are three kinds of people in this business. Dishonest people like that fellow," he gestured to the file in her hands, "who do whatever they please without considering the moral issue. Then there's the bulk of our workers," he gestured out his office window at the rows of cubicles in the main room, "people who keep their heads down, do their work, and never question anything. People who ignore problems that don't affect them directly, because they don't want to rock the boat. Those are the type of people who never get anywhere, because they're too afraid to take risks."

He folded his hands and leaned forward. "Then there are the risk takers. People who have conviction, and are willing to do what it takes to stand by what they believe in. People like you."

She stared at him, her mouth dry. She couldn't get her thoughts in order. "What are you saying?"

"I'm saying that you took a big risk, because you thought it was the right thing to do. Oh," he made a dismissive wave with one hand, "I suppose I should be mad at you for going behind my back. And I am, a bit. But then I think about what might have happened if there really had been a problem, if our products had been making someone sick, and if someone on the inside had been covering it up. That wasn't what happened this time, but that *has* happened before. And we need people with strong convictions to track down that sort of thing, uncover it, and report the truth."

Tessa licked her lips. She took a deep breath. "Mr. Morgan, are you saying...?"

"I'm saying I want to transfer you to QA." He leaned back in his chair. "You've been here, what, six, seven years? I've thought for awhile now that you were being wasted in data entry. You're a talented woman. But I never thought you had the moxie for real advancement. You've always stood in line with everyone else, like you were too afraid to stand out. Too afraid to rock the boat. Until now, that is."

Tessa shook her head. She couldn't process this. "So...instead of firing me, you're promoting me?"

"It's not a promotion," he said. "Not really. It's a transfer. But there will be a pay increase. QA has a lot more responsibility than Information Resources. And there's some travel involved. Sometimes you'll need to be flown out to some of our facilities around the country, to help with inspections."

"But I don't know anything about health inspections."

"You don't need to," he said. "What you need is spirit. The ability to stand up to people, to see past their bull and get at the truth. To analyze the data coming in from reports and find the discrepancies and the cover-ups. There's a sub-department in QA that takes care of the actual science, the testing and all that. But most of the staff is responsible for investigating the goings-on around the company and finding anything that needs to be fixed. And that's something I think you can do."

Tessa sat back in her chair. Her head was spinning so much that she wasn't sure she'd be able to stand. "I can't believe this."

"Believe it. Oh, there's just one thing."

She looked up at him, holding her breath. "Yes?"

"This situation?" He gestured between the two of them. "It stays between us. I still have to take care of that reporter, and I don't want word getting out that one of our employees was conducting an unauthorized investigation. It would give the media the wrong idea."

"Of course," she said. "I won't say anything."

"Good." He got up and walked her to the door, then shook her hand. "Take the rest of the day off. You look frazzled. Tomorrow morning I'll have the paperwork ready for you for the transfer. You'll need to fill out some new forms, so that payroll gets updated on your new position. That sort of thing."

"Yes. Of course. Thank you."

"Thank you, Tessa," he said. "For showing me that you've got moxie."

Tessa headed for the elevator, still in a daze. Mindy saw her exiting Mr. Morgan's office and she hurried over. "Hey, girl, what's going on?" She looked to Mr. Morgan as he closed his office door. "Are you in trouble or something? You're not getting sent home, are you?"

"No," Tessa said. "Not really." A grin spread on her lips.

"Then what happened?"

Tessa laughed. "Apparently, I'm finally moving up. You're looking at Dunham Enterprises' newest Quality Assurance Agent!"

Chapter Thirteen

Tessa went home, changed out of her nice suit and into jeans and a t-shirt, and poured herself a glass of wine. She was suddenly pent up with energy, and she needed an outlet for it. It was a beautiful, sunny day outside, so she grabbed her gardening supplies and headed out to tend her plot.

The seeds she had planted a few weeks ago were just beginning to sprout. She filled her watering can and gave them all a healthy drink, then tended to a few of the seedlings that needed her care. Most of the community was out today, including some people Tessa didn't usually see, since she was normally at work right now. Mrs. Mackenzie had made some homemade lemonade, and Tessa graciously accepted a glass. And while she stood in the sunshine sipping it, she looked across the way and saw Mr. Jones, out during the day for once, tending to his own little plot. It was no longer a Mystery Plot, though Tessa was still determined to one day solve the mystery of just how he got his crops to grow so beautifully.

The ringing of a bell called Tessa's attention to the other side of the garden, and she saw Samson riding his bike around the corner. He was dressed in his usual jeans, with an indie rock band t-shirt, and a bandana holding back his hair. He pedaled over to her, pulled out his iPod's earbuds, and gave her a concerned look.

"So, you got fired then?" he asked, no doubt expecting that to be the only reason she'd be home during the day.

"Actually," she said, handing him a glass of Mrs. Mackenzie's lemonade.

"That's an interesting story."

She told him all about her encounter with Mr. Morgan and how it had gone. He laughed and shook his head, clearly as flabbergasted as she had been. When she finished the story he said, "Wow. I guess it just goes to show you how much having the guts to stand up for yourself can pay off."

She looped her arm through his, and together they walked through the garden, admiring all of the new life growing all around them. And when Tessa passed by Topher's patch where he grew his award-winning zucchini, she didn't even think twice about the type of fertilizer he was using. She was determined from now on to keep her nose out of other people's business.

Except at her new job, of course. Where poking around to find out the truth was going to be what she did every day of the week.

THE END

Tessa's Summer

Chapter One

Tessa was working in her office on a hot, sweltering summer day when her neighbor Terry Jones unexpectedly called her.

"Tessa," he said, speaking with the same slow deliberation that he always did. "I'm sorry to bother you at work, but I think I need your help."

"Is something wrong?" Tessa asked. She held the phone between her head and her shoulder so she could keep typing the inspection report she was working on. Her workload at her new job had been overwhelming ever since the day she started, and it made it hard for her to focus on the phone call.

"Well, that's what I need your help with."

"I'm sorry?" Tessa asked, frowning.

"Well," Terry said, sighing into the phone. "I don't know if something is wrong. But if there is, I think you're the only person I can turn to."

Tessa bit her lip, looking at the clock on her computer. She only had about an hour left of work, and while she wasn't explicitly forbidden from taking personal calls in the office, it was frowned upon. Her boss would give her another lecture about how multitasking lowered productivity, and personal calls could wait until her personal time at home. "Is it something urgent?" she asked. "If not, I can stop by your place after I get done work and we can talk about it then. Would that work?"

"I suppose so," Terry said. "If it is what I think, it's been going on long enough that another couple of hours won't make much difference."

Tessa frowned at the ominousness of those words, but she didn't have time to question Terry further, because her manager walked in right at that moment. "Terry, I have to go, but I promise I'll come talk to you as soon as I can."

She quickly hung up and flashed a smile at Yvette Olivier, her immediate supervisor and head of the Quality Assurance Department at Dunham Enterprises. She wore a permanent scowl that Tessa and her coworkers had dubbed her "resting bitch face," not that they would ever say that to her face.

"I need you to drop everything else you're doing," Yvette said, handing her a thick manila folder. "There's an emergency recall that has to go out."

Tessa groaned as she took the folder

and opened it. "Seriously? Gosh, why do these things always have to come at the end of the day?"

"I'm sorry that our commitment to safety is incompatible with your busy social schedule," Yvette said, her cold expression never wavering. "Maybe you'd like it better back down in Information Resources?"

"No," Tessa said quickly, setting the folder on her desk. "No, it's fine. I'll take care of it." She'd been transferred from Information Resources to QA back in the spring, and it was far more satisfying work, and for better pay. She might not like it when she got stuck late in the office on days like this, but she really had come to love her job. Even if it was overwhelming at times.

"Those notices need to go out today, ASAP." Yvette pointed to the folder, giving Tessa a stern look. "And I'll need a followup on compliance first thing in the morning."

"Got it," Tessa said, trying not to grumble. Emergency product recalls were one of the most crucial parts of her job. They only happened when one of Dunham's products was found to be contaminated or dangerous in some way. Usually, they happened after a customer had called in a complaint, saying that they'd gotten sick from eating one of Dunham's products. Recalling all possible affected products was the only way to keep their customers safe, not to mention protecting Dunham from possible lawsuits.

She was stuck at the office for the next couple of hours, sending out notifications to their distributors and to any grocery stores that stocked their products. Most of it was precautionary.

The recall was due to a batch of apples that had allegedly made a few people sick, which required an investigation to find out if the issue had been caused in the orchards, or during shipping, or due to improper handling and refrigeration by the stores themselves. If it turned out the supermarket was to blame, then the recall would turn out to be unnecessary, since none of the other locations would be at risk. But until they found out for sure, they had to recall all potentially affected products from everywhere in the region.

Fortunately, Dunham's online systems made it easy to send out recall notices en masse. But Tessa still had to backtrack the shipping numbers to find out exactly which batches were potentially at risk, making sure she sent the recalls only to the correct locations.

By the time she finished, it was getting late, and most of the rest of the office had already gone home. In the morning, Tessa would have to check for responses from the management at each distribution center and supermarket to get confirmation of the recall, then send out second notices to anyone who hadn't complied. Meanwhile, all she wanted to do was go home, open a bottle of wine, and spend the rest of the night relaxing.

On the drive home, she felt for sure that she was forgetting something. She wracked her mind, trying to remember what it was, but after hours of work, it had completely slipped her mind.

When she pulled into the parking lot of her apartment complex at home, there was an ambulance parked outside. Red and blue lights bathed the building in their harsh glow, and a crowd of Tessa's neighbors was gathered outside.

She got out of her car and headed for the building, her heart racing as she feared for the friends she had in the building, and for her boyfriend, Samson, who lived right down the hall from her. She pushed her way to the front of the crowd and got there just as the EMTs were wheeling out a stretcher.

She got as close as she could before

one of the EMTs pushed her back. "I'm sorry ma'am, give us some room."

She stepped back, her face going white as she looked at the man on the stretcher. The deep-set lines on his weathered brown face showed the signs of a life that had been long and wearisome, though Tessa was used to seeing a quiet, content smile on his face. She had never before seen him wracked with pain and struggling for breath.

"Terry," she whispered, watching in horror as they loaded him into the ambulance. She stepped forward, reaching for him. "Wait, I know him. He just—"

"Ma'am, we need to get him to the hospital, now. You can come down there to check on him if you like, but we need to go."

She licked her lips, unsure what to say or do. She almost told them to wait, that she might know something, but she realized she didn't have any idea what she *did* know. Just that he had said he needed her help, but she didn't know what kind of help she could have offered.

She stood there with the rest of the crowd and watched as Terry was taken away. Her gut churned with fear for him, and with guilt for having completely forgotten about his call.

She got back into her car and drove after the ambulance. She didn't know what help she could possibly be, but Terry had called her, and told her she was the only one he could turn to. She couldn't ignore that.

She just hoped that whatever was going on, she wasn't too late to do something about it.

Chapter Two

Tessa was only a short distance behind the ambulance, but she fell behind because the traffic that parted for the ambulance started closing back in before she could get by. She blared on her horn and tried to find a way around the traffic, but she ended up stuck behind a line of cars. By the time she reached the hospital, Terry had already been taken into the emergency room.

She walked up to the woman behind the front counter, a tall blonde lady not much older than Tessa was. Tessa drummed her fingers nervously on the counter and said "I need to talk to someone about the man that was just brought in here. African American male, elderly, he should have just come through."

"Just one moment," the woman said. She checked something in the computer, then stepped aside to speak to a doctor. When she returned, she gestured to the waiting room. "They're looking at him now. You can wait here."

"You don't understand," Tessa said. "He called me not long before he...before he collapsed. He told me something was wrong."

"Do you know what caused his collapse?"

"Well," Tessa said, wringing her hands, "no. But he was calling me for help. He said I was the only one he could turn to."

"Did you call for an ambulance?"

"No...no." Tessa shook her head, tears welling in his eyes. "I didn't know there was something *wrong*, exactly. He just said he needed help."

The woman frowned at her. Tessa looked away, fearing her judgment. If she had known Terry was in any kind of danger, she would have called for help. She only wished she hadn't been delayed at work. If the delay had led to Terry's collapse...

"Wait here please," the woman said. She stepped through a door to the side, and Tessa was left waiting there, alone with her guilt.

A few minutes later, a doctor came out of the ER and started asking her questions. She was unable to give him anything more than half-answers.

"Do you know if he has any medical conditions? Drug allergies?"

"Not that I know of." She chewed on her lip, trying to think of something that could help. She'd only been friends with Terry for a few months.

"When he called you, did he mention any symptoms? Anything that can give us a clue about what happened?"

"No. I didn't even think it was something medical. He just said he needed my help. Do you know what's wrong with him?"

"We have him on an IV drip right now," the doctor said. "He's showing signs of nausea, severe dehydration, and heat exhaustion. He's going to need to be under observation for awhile. Do you know if he has any family that should be contacted?"

"No. Not that I know of." Tessa only knew bits and pieces about Terry's life. She knew he'd been in jail for a number of years, and that he had lived an isolated life since he got out. The impression she'd been under was that any family he had were either deceased, or no longer speaking to him. She thought back over the conversations she'd had with him, and realized she didn't know much about him. "He once told me he used to have a drug problem, but I think that was a long time ago."

The doctor pulled out a pen and made some notes on the chart. "Do you know what kind of drugs?"

"No, I'm sorry."

"All right." He put his pen back in his pocket and turned to leave. "We'll keep you informed. But it might be some time before he regains consciousness."

"Okay." Tessa's shoulders slumped. She went to sit in the waiting room, not sure what else to do. She just knew she couldn't leave without knowing if Terry was going to be okay. Without any family, or even any close friends that she knew of, he would be all alone here in the hospital. She couldn't leave him alone like that.

She lost track of time sitting there, until she heard someone call her name. She looked up and saw her boyfriend, Samson, crossing the waiting room. He was dressed in his usual "hipster hippie" look, with tight jeans, an indie rock band t-shirt, and a headband holding back his long hair.

She stood up and stepped into his

arms. He held her tight, stroking her hair. "I heard what happened. Mrs. Mackenzie said she saw you chasing after the ambulance. Is Terry okay?"

She explained everything the doctor had said, then told Samson about the phone call from Terry. "I just don't understand. He said that whatever it was, it had been going on a long time. But I can't imagine what he could have been talking about. And why call me?"

"Do you think it could have something to do with your work?" Samson asked.

Tessa thought about that, touching her fingers to her lips. Her work in Dunham's QA department meant that she dealt with a lot of food safety issues. Dunham was a company known for supplying clean, healthy, organic foods, though she'd learned while working there that there were occasionally problems. Problems like the recall she'd been working on earlier, which the company tried to keep hush-hush. They were committed to safety, but also to secrecy, in order to protect the company's reputation.

"I don't see how it could have anything to do with Dunham," Tessa said. "I mean, Terry mostly ate food he grew himself in his garden."

"Do you think there could be something wrong with the gardens?" Samson asked.

"Gosh...do you think that could be it?" Tessa put a hand over her mouth, her face going pale. Tessa, Samson, and a number of their neighbors ran a community garden on the plot of land between two apartment buildings. Each tenant had their own little plot, growing everything from herbs to flowers to fresh produce. Everything was supposed to be organic, and the community had strict rules against using chemicals or anything artificial, in order to keep everything growing healthy and pure. But if something had gotten into the garden...

"I still think Topher has been using something that's against the rules," Samson said, frowning. "Some kind of harsh herbicide or pesticide. The little rat is so sneaky about it. I've never much cared for him."

"Yeah, but do you really think he could have contaminated Terry's crops?" Tessa shook her head. "That doesn't seem like him."

"He wouldn't do it on purpose." Samson crossed his arms. "But if you let some stuff get into the groundwater, it can spread. Something that affects one person's plot could affect the whole garden."

Tessa thought back over everything Terry had said. He'd told her that whatever it was, it had been going on for awhile. Had he discovered something harmful in the community's garden?

If that was the case, Tessa realized, then all of their neighbors could be at risk. Tessa herself grew tomatoes and watermelons, along with a few other things. Though she never could seem to get her tomatoes to grow as big and ripe as some of her neighbors did, particularly Topher.

She traded with all of her neighbors for a wide variety of fresh fruits and vegetables. She'd shared quite a bit with Terry over the last few months, since they'd become friends. Which meant if he'd gotten sick because of something in his food, then Tessa, Samson, and all of the others could have been affected as well.

"I think I need to sit down," Tessa said, touching a hand to her head. The room started to spin.

Samson helped her to a chair. "I'll get the doctor."

As soon as he had her settled in her seat, he hurried over to speak to someone about getting both of them checked. Tessa just sat and stared, unable to get her mind around what was happening. Her stomach was twisted in knots and her mouth had suddenly gone dry.

By the time a doctor came over to check on her, she felt like she was about to pass out. She just silently hoped that it was only caused by the stress, and not by some unknown toxin that she could have been eating for months on end.

Chapter Three

Tessa spent a couple of hours in the hospital. The doctors drew blood, had her pee in a cup, and asked her a bunch of questions about her diet and her daily habits. They also made sure to ask about anything she had in common with Terry. She explained all about the community gardening plot, while the doctor's took notes.

"Has anyone else in your apartment complex been sick lately?" the doctor asked.

"No," Tessa said, shaking her head. "Not that I know of. And I was feeling fine until I came down here."

"When was the last time you ate?"

"Well, I..." Tessa stopped and thought about it. She realized that between being stuck at work late, then rushing down to the hospital, she hadn't eaten dinner. And she'd been so busy at work that her lunch had been some orange juice and a mini bag of pretzels from the vending machine. "Well, I guess I haven't had much since breakfast."

"That would easily explain your dizziness." The doctor made some notes on her chart. "I don't think you're in any danger. We're still going to run your blood work just to be sure. We'll have the results in a couple of days. But you should be all right to go home, as long as you get your blood sugar up first."

She was discharged soon after and met up with Samson, who had also been given a clean bill of health. Before they left the hospital, Tessa asked the doctor, "Can we see Terry before we go?"

"He's sleeping right now," the doctor said. "He came to for a few minutes earlier, but he was still a bit out of it. I'd rather not have him disturbed. You can stop by tomorrow to check up on him. Now that we're getting some fluids in him, he should be all right after some rest."

"All right. Thank you, doctor."

The doctor gave her his card so she could check with him for further updates. Tessa and Samson headed home, and when they got there Tessa invited Samson into her apartment so they could unwind together after the stressful night. Samson made some tea from the herbs he grew in his garden plot. He handed her the steaming mug and sat with her on the sofa, pulling her feet into his lap. "So, what do you think we should do?" he asked.

Tessa leaned back on the cushions while Samson pulled off her shoes and started rubbing her aching feet. She laid there for a few minutes with her eyes closed, inhaling the aroma of the tea. "Well, I want to talk to Terry first. Find out what he called me about. I'd rather not jump to any conclusions like last time."

Samson laughed, shaking his head. "Yeah, that was a bit of a fiasco. But it all worked out in the end."

"This time we might not be so lucky," she said. It had been a few months since Tessa's unauthorized investigation into one of the distribution centers at Dunham Enterprises. She'd thought that someone at her company had been covering up a health hazard. It had turned out to be a red herring, and she had nearly lost her job by crossing lines and taking matters into her own hands, instead of letting the right people handle it. Though now that she was working for QA, she was the right person.

"If there is a problem with the gardens," she said, "I can bring samples down to one of Dunham's labs."

"Will they let you do that?" Samson asked. "I don't want to get you in trouble. We can always ask my friend

Gregory instead. I'm sure he'd run some tests as a favor."

Tessa nodded. "That might be best. Though in any case, I don't want to do anything until we know more." She looked out the window at the darkened gardens. There was no one out there at this time of night, and the gardens were basked in shadows broken only by the dim lights coming from the apartment windows. "I don't want to scare any of our neighbors. If they know we're testing the crops for chemicals or other contaminants, people might freak out."

"But if there is something wrong," Samson said, "they have the right to know."

"They do." Tessa sipped her tea, letting the warmth soothe her throat. "And as soon as we know whether there's something to tell them, we'll let everyone know. I'll head to the hospital first thing tomorrow—darn."

"What is it?" Samson looked up at her

with a concerned frown.

"I forgot I have some important work to do tomorrow. I can't put it off."

"Don't worry." He shifted closer to her on the couch, pulling her legs across his lap. He leaned over and kissed her forehead. "I'm off tomorrow. I'll head down to the hospital first thing in the morning, and check in on Terry."

"All right." She smiled up at him and caressed his cheek. They sat there together in quiet comfort for awhile. Their relationship was still new, but she felt like they were settling into a nice, comfortable routine together. They'd been friends for years before they took things a step further, so it had been a natural transition.

They still spent their weekends and afternoons together in the garden, or they went on nature hikes or wine tastings. They spent most evenings together, except for nights when Samson had shifts at the music shop he worked at. It was a pleasant, simple relationship, and so far Tessa had been grateful for a relationship without all the drama that she'd had with some men in the past.

She set her tea on the coffee table and leaned against Samson. He wrapped his arm around her shoulder and they snuggled together, her head laying against his shoulder. They stayed there like that until Tessa started to drift off to sleep at which time she knew she had to go home.

Tessa got up and stretched. She had felt so warm and snuggly that she didn't want to get up, but she knew she had to get to work early in the morning. She laid a blanket over Samson to let him sleep. Since he tended to work a lot of nights at the music shop, it was unusual for him to fall asleep on the sofa. Besides, he looked so cute when he was sleeping. His hair was half out of its usual ponytail and he had a peaceful look on his face. She gave him a kiss on the forehead, then drowsily made her way to her own apartment.

Chapter Four

The next day, Tessa spent most of her morning sorting through the emails she'd gotten from various supermarkets and distribution centers, confirming the recall. She updated the database to keep track of which locations had complied and which ones she was still waiting for replies from, then she sent out a round of second notices to any that hadn't responded. She also forwarded the information on the recall to the department responsible for inventory and logistics, so they could account for the amount of product that was being removed from the market.

By the end of the day, there were shipments of thousands upon thousands of apples being sent back to Dunham

TESSA'S SUMMER

Enterprises. Some of them would be subject to testing to discover what the problem was. The rest would be destroyed to make sure no one was at risk from eating a potentially contaminated product.

After work, she headed straight for the hospital. She got a visitor's pass and headed for Terry's room. Samson was there, sitting by the side of the bed, talking to Terry. Though when she walked into the room, Tessa saw that Terry was unconscious.

"Hey," Samson said, rising from his seat and giving her a hug.

"Hey. How's he doing?"

"He's been in and out of consciousness. The doctor said he's going to be fine. They're just trying to get his blood pressure back up. He should be okay to go home tomorrow, maybe."

"That's good." She reached over and patted Terry's hand. He stirred a bit, his eyes struggling to open. "Has he said anything yet about what happened?"

"Not yet. He tried, but he's lost his voice. They gave him something to help soothe his throat and help his vocal chords mend."

Tessa sighed, still trying to figure out what Terry might have called her about.

"Listen," Samson said, "I've got to get going. I'm due at work. But I'll check in when I get done, okay?"

"All right." Tessa gave him a quick kiss, then took the chair by the bed. Terry was still fading in and out of consciousness. She squeezed his hand. "Terry? It's me, Tessa. How are you feeling?"

He raised a weak hand and touched it to his lips. Tessa looked around and saw a plastic cup sitting on the table by the bed. She held it up and helped get the straw between Terry's lips. He took a small drink, then started coughing. She grabbed some tissues to help wipe off his chin.

"Terry, you called me yesterday. Do you remember?"

Terry nodded, his movements slow and weak.

"You said there was something wrong. Something I could help you with. Do you remember what it was?"

Terry nodded and opened his mouth to speak, but he could only wheeze and cough. He looked up at her, the strain clear in his eyes. Then he made a gesture with his hand.

She watched the way his hand was moving, not sure what he was trying to say. Then she realized he was making a writing motion. "You want to write it down?"

He nodded.

Tessa dug into her purse and pulled out a small notepad and a couple of pens. She held them out to Terry. He took the black pen first, then dropped it and took the red one instead. She held the notepad up while he drew the pen across it, drawing a red circle.

Tessa frowned at it. She didn't understand what he was trying to say. Then he started scribbling the pen across the circle, filling it in with red.

"What is that?" she asked. The shape was crude, and Terry's hand was shaking. He took the black pen and made a mark near the top of the circle. Then he ran out of strength and laid back on the pillow, letting out a long sigh.

Tessa took the notebook and studied the crude drawing. The black mark near the top looked like some kind of leaf or stem. Which made the drawing look like a piece of fruit.

"An apple?" She looked up at Terry, but he had fallen back to sleep.

Her mind went straight to the recall of Dunham apples. She didn't know if Terry bought any Dunham produce. He mostly grew his own fruit and vegetables in his garden, but of course he didn't have an apple tree. He'd have to buy those at the supermarket.

She tried to gently wake him, but he was deep asleep. On top of that, visiting hours would be ending soon.

She looked around the room, then opened the drawer in the little table by the bed. Terry's things, whatever had been in his pockets when he was brought to the hospital, were there in a labeled plastic bag. She tore open the bag and took out his keys, watching over her shoulder to make sure the doctor didn't see her.

Technically, what she was doing was illegal, but since Terry didn't have any family, there was no one else who could help.

She left the room and found the doctor, asking him a few questions. What she learned didn't make her feel any better.

"He's been suffering from some

diarrhea and vomiting," the doctor said. "That might be part of the cause of his dehydration. It's likely that this was a case of food poisoning. Do you know anything about his diet? I know you mentioned something about a community garden."

"He grows most of his own produce," Tessa said. "Though most of our neighbors trade fruits and vegetables. It could have come from anywhere."

"Well, there's not necessarily any cause for alarm. It could have come from some undercooked meat, from milk or cheese, or from raw produce. The symptoms aren't usually this severe, but due to Mr. Jones's age, and his history of low blood pressure, it hit him especially hard. If any of your neighbors start to show any symptoms, you should suggest they get checked out. In mild cases, they might just need plenty of bed rest and fluids, but you don't want to take any chances."

"Thank you, doctor."

Tessa headed home and changed out of her work clothes, then she headed down the hall to Terry's apartment. She checked up and down the hall to make sure none of her neighbors saw her going into his apartment. She was confident that Terry would be okay with her doing this, under the circumstances, but some of her neighbors could be nosy, and they might get the wrong idea.

She unlocked the door and slipped inside. Even after she flipped on the lights, the apartment was dim and subdued. The furniture was old, worn, and mismatched, but there was a cozy feeling to the place.

She headed for the kitchen and looked in Terry's refrigerator. It was filled with a lot of Terry's homegrown carrots, potatoes, berries, and tomatoes. There was a pot of some kind of leftover stew, and a couple of containers of some kind of takeout food. And on the bottom shelf there was a plastic bag filled with half a dozen apples.

Tessa pulled it out and ripped the bag open. She pulled out one of the apples and held it up under the light. The little sticker on the side was marked with the logo of Dunham Enterprises.

Chapter Five

"But Dunham did a recall, right?" Samson asked after she explained the situation to him. "I mean, they're handling it. Assuming this is even what made Terry sick."

"I don't know." Tessa threw up her hands, then started pacing around Samson's apartment. It was late at night, and Samson had just gotten home from work. "I mean, I'm the one who sent out the recalls. So, yes, it's being handled. But I still feel..."

"Responsible?" Samson asked.

Tessa sighed. Her shoulders slumped. She stared out the window at the garden plots. She hadn't had time to tend to her tomatoes and watermelons for a few days. She'd only briefly checked on them earlier, and they had looked shriveled and pathetic.

"I'm sure there's no one to blame, really," she said. "The internal investigation hasn't found any signs of negligence. It could have been something as simple as poor refrigeration in one of the trucks, or a worker somewhere who forgot to wash their hands after they went to the bathroom. Which might be gross, but it's hardly criminal."

"So, what do you want to do?"

Tessa stared out the window, not sure what to say. It didn't seem like there was anything to do. Terry was going to be fine. She'd thrown the rest of the apples in the trash, just to be on the safe side. As far as she could figure, it was simply case closed, nothing else to be done. Sure, Terry had the option of seeking a legal settlement with Dunham for his medical bills, though for all she knew, the supermarket had been the ones to mishandle the produce. Most likely, nothing would happen, and Terry would be good as new within a few days.

Though none of that stopped Tessa from feeling the pangs of guilt.

Samson stepped up behind her and wrapped his arms around her. "Maybe you should try to keep your mind off it. You have tomorrow off, right? Spend the day in your garden. I'll be right there with you. And I'll bet Mrs. Mackenzie will make some of her famous lemonade."

Tessa sighed and leaned back against Samson. He was right. She needed to relax.

She spent the night at Samson's, and in the morning, they headed out to tend their gardens. It was a hot, sunny day, and quite a few of their neighbors were out as well. Mrs. Mackenzie had made a jug of lemonade, and Tessa had a glass in between tending to her poor, shriveled tomatoes.

She knelt in the dirt and worked on mixing some more organic fertilizer, hoping her crummy little crops would do better. She couldn't figure out what was wrong with them this year. The heat wave might have been drying them out, though she made sure to water them regularly. And Topher's tomatoes were certainly doing just fine.

She watched him from across the garden. Topher always kept to himself, and he had this strange habit of muttering to himself while he worked. The only word she could think of to describe him was "twitchy." And yet, despite his strangeness, he grew the best crops in the entire garden. She could see from here as he tended to his tomato vines. They were plump and ripe and the size of his fist.

He looked up and caught her staring. He immediately moved around with his back to her, blocking her view of his tomatoes. She scoffed and shook her head. *As if I want to know your great gardening secrets, Topher.*

After they'd spent some time tending to their plots, Samson came over and said, "Hey, maybe we should take care of Terry's plot, too. He's been away for a couple of days now."

"Yeah, good idea. I don't think he'd mind if we did a little weeding and watering."

"I think he's supposed to be coming home later today," Samson said. "When we get done, we should head down there and see if he needs a ride. Or at least a little 'welcome home' gathering. It'd be a shame for the poor guy to get out of the hospital and find out there's no one there to meet him."

Tessa smiled. Samson was always so considerate. It was one of the things that had drawn her to him. "You're wonderful, you know that?"

"Who, me?" He smirked and shook his head. "Naww."

"Yes." She wrapped her arms around him and kissed him, not caring that they were both still wearing their gardening gloves and getting dirt everywhere.

They both knelt down to start digging up weeds. Then while Samson watered the plot, Tessa took out her gardening shears and started trimming some of the dead leaves off a few of the plants. She noticed some of his plants were shriveled as badly as hers. The leaves were wilting, and some of the stems and vines were limp and lifeless. She couldn't tell if it was only due to a few days of neglect, or if there were something else going on. The damage was the worst at the top of the plants, and on tomatoes that had grown vertically on the trellises throughout the garden. Nearer to the ground, everything seemed fine.

She made a mental note to ask Terry about the damage, and to Google for some answers later on. When she and

Samson finished tending the garden, Tessa headed home to shower, then changed into clean clothes to go out and pick up Terry. She and Samson drove down to the hospital together, and they stopped at the gift shop before heading upstairs. They bought a pot of azaleas, and after a short but intense debate about whether Terry was too old for it, a "Get Well Soon" balloon with Sesame Street characters on it.

"You're never too old for Grover," Samson said as they checked out. Tessa just laughed and shook her head.

When they got upstairs, they found Terry sitting on the edge of the hospital bed, tying his shoes. He still looked weak and a bit under the weather, but he was up and about, and that sent a wave of relief through Tessa. "Terry," she said. "I'm so glad you're feeling better."

They gave Terry the gifts. A beaming smile spread on his face. "Well, I never expected such courtesy. Thank you.

Thank you so much."

He laughed at the balloon, and examined the azaleas with a gardener's critical eye. They chatted a bit, and he told them everything the doctors had said before they released him.

"Didn't mean to frighten anyone," he said with a bashful grin. "Must have been something I ate." He patted his stomach, then winced, clearly still feeling a bit nauseous.

"Don't worry, Terry," Tessa said. "I checked in on your garden and your apartment, and I threw those apples out."

She pulled his keys out of her purse and handed them over. He took them, looking up at her with a confused expression.

"Apples?" he asked. "Tessa, what are you talking about?"

"The apples in your fridge. They were bad. I threw them out."

Terry scratched his head. "You threw

out my apples? I hadn't even had any yet."

Tessa and Samson exchanged a look.

"Terry," Tessa said. "When I was here before, and I asked you what was wrong, you drew a picture of an apple."

"Oh, no," Terry said, shaking his head. "No, Tessa, there's nothing wrong with the apples. I was trying to tell you."

He made a fist, his jaw taking on a determined set. "I think something's wrong with my tomatoes!"

Chapter Six

While they took the elevator downstairs, Tessa asked Terry about what was going on.

"So, you ate a bad tomato, and that's what got you sick?" She frowned, though she was glad at least that it had nothing to do with her job.

"Bad tomatoes? Heck no!" Terry laughed and slapped his knee. "Tessa, girl, you get some funny ideas. No, I think it was the sushi I ate the other night that set me off. Didn't mean to put a scare in you."

"I'm confused," Samson said. "So, what do the tomatoes have to do with anything?"

"That's what I called Tessa for," Terry said. "What, did you think I called you because I was getting sick? Why would I call you instead of a doctor?"

Tessa rubbed her hand across her face. She silently reminded herself to stop jumping to conclusions, and to actually get all the information before she started panicking next time.

They got off the elevator and headed outside to the car. "Terry," Tessa said, "why don't you just explain what's going on? Then maybe we can see if we can help."

"Well, I don't know if you've looked at my crops lately, but my tomatoes are looking really sad. I happened to take a look at yours, and they're having the same problem. But I took a walk around the gardens, and it looks like almost everyone else is doing just fine. But yours and mine, they're almost right next to each other. So, I figured we've got the same problem."

They got into Tessa's car. "Well," she said, letting out a sigh of relief, "I'm glad all you were calling me about was gardening tips. I was going to do some research this weekend, see if I can find out what the trouble might be."

"I've already got a theory on that," Terry said. "You know everyone talks about Topher, about his fancy, award-winning veggies."

Samson snorted. "Yeah, I've never much liked him. He always looks like he's up to something."

"But do you have anything more than suspicions?" Tessa asked as she drove out of the parking lot.

"I've seen him spraying something around his plot," Terry said. His jaw set in a righteous scowl. "Don't know what it is. He says it's all organic. But you know the way the wind gets funneled between the apartment buildings? Well, your plot and mine, we're usually downwind of Topher. Whatever he's spraying, I think it's getting carried onto our tomatoes."

"But if he's spraying something harmful," Tessa said, "how come his crops are doing fine?"

"Whatever he uses, he sprays it down on the weeds. Makes sure not to get anything on his plants. But then the wind picks it up, carries it over to our tomatoes." Terry shook his head, rapping a fist against his knee. "Just gets my goat, it does. He knows the rules, same as everyone else. But he gets so smug."

When Tessa pulled the car up to a traffic light, she turned around in her seat to look at Terry. "So, what do you think we should do?"

"Do you want to get the crops tested?" Samson suggested.

"Wouldn't matter if we got them tested," Terry said. "We'd have to be able to prove it was him that did it. And even then, what could we do? He's not breaking any laws. Not really. Just our community rules."

Tessa turned back around, lost in thought. The light turned green and she started driving, trying to sort through the thoughts in her head. Terry was right. Technically speaking, using chemical pesticides and weed killers wasn't illegal. If they tried to bring Topher to court—assuming he was even the one responsible, since all they had were suspicions—they'd have to somehow prove willful negligence, showing that his use of chemicals was harming their plots. And since the combined value of Tessa and Terry's garden plots was negligible, at least on a monetary scale, they'd be hard pressed to prove they were owed anything. It wouldn't be worth the time and effort to get the courts involved to replace the value of a few tomato plants.

No, pursuing this matter legally would be a waste of time. This was a community matter. The only thing Topher might be guilty of was breaking the community rules and lying to them all. And while that irritated Tessa quite a bit, it wouldn't be anything more than a personal grudge.

"The first thing we need to do," she said, drumming her fingers on the steering wheel, "is find out if Topher is even the one responsible. Chemical contamination could have come from anywhere. If we can prove that it's him, then we can see what to do about it."

"So how do we do that?" Samson asked.

"I've been keeping an eye on him for awhile now," Terry said. "Problem is, everything he uses is a homemade mixture. Not like we can look through his garbage for a can of RoundUp."

"So, we get our hands on some of his herbicides," Tessa said. "Find out what's in it."

"And then?" Samson asked.

"One step at a time," Tessa said. "I don't want to get ahead of ourselves. We find out the truth, first thing, and worry about the rest later."

"Sounds good to me," Terry said. "Only question is, how are you going to get some of his herbicide? You'll need to get some before he sprays it. If we just test the soil, we wouldn't know anything. Like you said, contamination could come from anywhere."

"Easy," Tessa said, grinning. "We'll just pull ourselves a little heist."

Chapter Seven

They discussed the plan that night in Terry's apartment, over tea and biscuits. The next day was Sunday, one of the biggest gardening days in the community. Most of their neighbors were off work, and other than a few of them that went to church in the morning, they mostly spent their mornings outdoors, tending to their gardens and enjoying the fresh air and sunshine.

Tessa and Samson were out early Sunday morning, tending to their gardens. Samson was watering the herbs he kept in a line of clay pots, while Tessa was trimming the withered leaves from her tomato plants, hoping to somehow salvage what was left of them.

She tossed the clippings in a plastic bucket, while keeping an eye out for Terry to make his move.

Around mid-morning, Topher came out, carrying his gardening tools and a bucket of herbicide with a spray nozzle attached. When he bragged to the neighborhood about his award-winning crops, he always claimed that he used a fertilizer made from a mixture of ground kelp and water, and an all-natural herbicide made from a mixture of ground oranges in citrus oil. Tessa watched from her plot as he set the sprayer down and started trimming some dead leaves. He glanced over his shoulder constantly while he worked, and he didn't talk to anyone. He even turned down Mrs. Mackenzie when she came over to offer him a glass of lemonade.

Terry glanced over at Tessa and she nodded, giving him the signal to go. He grabbed his bucket of clippings and started heading for the compost heap. Part way there, he tripped and spilled his bucket, spreading leaves and crud all over some of Topher's plants.

"Aww, man! Come on, Mr. Jones, I just weeded that!" Topher ran his fingers through his hair, grumbling under his breath.

"Sorry, son," Terry said. He straightened up and stretched out his back, putting on a good show of looking like a tired old man. "It's just so hard to keep a good grip on things these days. I don't suppose you could lend an old fella a hand?"

Topher glanced around, and saw that Tessa was watching him. She quickly lowered her head, acting like she was minding her own business. Topher turned back to Terry, still grumbling. "Yeah, sure, whatever," he said. He knelt down and started scooping the spilled clippings back into the bucket, then carried it off to the compost heap.

As soon as he was out of sight around the corner, Tessa and Samson made their move. Keeping an eye out to make sure none of their neighbors was watching, they hurried over to Topher's plot. Tessa unscrewed the top of the sprayer while Samson held out a plastic cup. They poured some of the liquid herbicide in, then Tessa struggled to get the cap back on the sprayer.

She glanced over and saw Topher and Terry returning. Her heart started to race. She fumbled with the cap of the sprayer, but it wouldn't quite go on.

Samson came to the rescue by hurrying over to Topher and distracting him. "Hey, Topher, man. Lemme ask you something."

He stepped in the other direction so that Topher had to turn his back on Tessa in order to talk to him. They chatted for a brief moment, giving Tessa time to screw the cap back on the sprayer. She grabbed the cup with the sample and headed back to her plot, hiding the cup in with her gardening supplies.

"Dude, I'm busy, okay?" Topher said, turning away from Samson. He headed back to his plot and knelt down, grumbling and sorting through his tools.

Tessa glanced back and caught Samson's eye. He winked at her. They went about their business until enough time had passed that they wouldn't seem suspicious, then they headed inside, bringing the ill-gotten sample with them.

Once they were inside Tessa's apartment, she gave the cup to Samson. "Did you already call your friend at the university?" she asked.

"Yup." Samson held the cup up to the light, looking at the way the light shone through the dark liquid. If there's anything in here besides oranges, he should be able to let us know within a couple of days."

"Tell him I said thanks," Tessa said. She pulled off her gardening gloves and stretched her back. "Though I don't know what I'll do if this turns out to be another false alarm. I'm going to feel bad if we keep taking up Gregory's time over nothing."

"He doesn't mind." Samson gave her a wink. "He told me it's more exciting than his usual work. Apparently it's just as boring doing the actual lab work, but it makes him feel like he's part of some secret conspiracy to expose the truth."

Tessa laughed, throwing her arms around Samson's neck. "Ha! The secret gardening conspiracy. If only it were something so exciting. I just don't want my tomatoes to wilt."

He put his arms around her waist and kissed her. She stared up into his eyes. "Why do you put up with me?" she asked. "I mean, I'm always dragging you into these crazy schemes."

"Maybe I like crazy schemes," he said.

"It sure beats going to work on Sunday."

"Crazy man." She pulled him close and kissed him again, and this time, she didn't let go.

Chapter Eight

The next couple of days were mostly uneventful. Tessa's days at the office were spent following up on the recall. She got reports back from the labs and found out that the contaminated apples had, in fact, been isolated to a single supermarket. While they couldn't be sure how the contamination had happened, it was clear that someone at that supermarket wasn't following proper food safety procedures.

She sent notifications to all of the other supermarkets and facilities letting them know that the recall was over, and she sent an official notice to the one affected supermarket requiring updated safe food handling procedures and retraining of all personnel.

Compliance with Dunham's corporate standards was a requirement of doing business with them, so the supermarket would have to either get their procedures up to par, or risk losing Dunham as a supplier.

She was so overloaded with all the paperwork involved that she almost forgot about the Topher situation. She was stuck late at work one night, finishing up some reports, when she remembered that she'd forgotten to eat again. She was feeling a bit dizzy, and decided she needed to get something to eat before she headed home. Maybe even something a bit greasy, since every once in awhile she got tired of always eating healthy and organic.

She hit a fast food drive thru on the way home and walked into the apartment building carrying a bag of food and drinking a vanilla milkshake. She'd already eaten the burger in the car, and was looking forward to scarfing down the french fries with a glass of wine, and she didn't care how much those flavors would clash.

When she got to her apartment, she found a note on the door, written in Samson's handwriting. It said he had a surprise for her at his place.

She rolled her eyes at his romantic corniness and headed down the hall. She walked in without knocking; they'd both spent so much time at each other's apartments over the past few months that they'd gotten used to having open invitations to each other's homes. When she walked in, she saw Samson sitting on the sofa, reading a book and looking bored. On the other side of the room was a table made up with a dinner for two, complete with a bottle of wine and two candles that were burned most of the way down.

"Aww," she said, looking at the scene before her. "Was this for me?"

"Shoot." Samson quickly got up and

set his book aside, then straightened his clothes. He was normally a t-shirt and jeans kind of guy, but he'd gone all out tonight with khakis and a button-down shirt. She even saw a pair of leather loafers sitting by the couch, though Samson was barefoot now.

"Oh no," Tessa said, setting her milkshake and bag on the table. "Did I ruin it? If I'd known you had something planned, I wouldn't have stayed at work so late!"

"Well if you'd known about it," Samson said, smirking and putting his arms around her, "it wouldn't have been a surprise."

"Silly." She playfully smacked him on the chest, then laid her head against him. "Next time, call me and, I dunno, trick me into coming home early."

"I'll fake a heart attack," he said. "I know then you'll come running."

"Don't joke about that." She smacked his chest again, harder this time. "I'd just about lose it if you wound up in the hospital."

"Really?" he asked, looking down at her with a curious smile on his face.

She blushed and turned away. "Of course."

"I guess I just wasn't sure you felt that strongly for me."

"Do I not make that clear?" she asked. She looked up at him, pouting. "You know I care about you, right?"

"I hope so." He stroked her hair, looking into her eyes.

"I must not say it enough, then." She sighed and pulled him close, her head pressed against his chest. "You're a sweet, kind, caring man. You make me smile. And I haven't been this happy in a very long time."

He kissed the top of her head. "Well, you're going to give a guy a big head."

She giggled, then peeked over Samson's shoulder to look at the table. "Can we still have dinner? Or did I ruin it by having a burger first?"

He held her chair out for her and poured them each a glass of wine, then fetched dinner from the fridge. He'd made shrimp salad, with some kind of sweet little fruit cakes for dessert. They drank wine and ate, talking and joking about life and all of its ups and downs. They didn't once bring up the issue with Topher and the mysteriously wilting tomatoes, and it felt nice for Tessa to have a night where she had no worries and everything felt carefree.

After dinner they sat together on the couch, Tessa sitting between Samson's legs and leaning back against his chest. They watched as the candles burned down to almost nothing, content to hold each other in comfortable silence.

Finally, Tessa said, "You keep this sort of thing up, I might just have to keep you around."

"Oh?" Samson chuckled. "And here I thought you only liked me for my herbal teas."

She laughed and nuzzled against him. "I mean it."

"Good," he said. "Because I'm not planning on going anywhere."

Tessa set down her wine glass and closed her eyes, letting her man hold her while her thoughts started to drift off. She thought about the future, wondering where all of this was headed. She hadn't given it much thought before now, with how busy her life had been. She was just content to have Samson there each day and night. Though maybe, she thought, they were heading down a path that was leading them to something more serious.

Maybe, she thought. But her thoughts were too scattered now, and all she could focus on was how warm it felt in Samson's arms, and how right at that moment, there was no place else in the world she would rather be.

Chapter Nine

The next day at work, while she was writing up her final reports on the results of the product recall, Tessa got a phone call from Samson's professor friend, Gregory.

"Hey, Gregory," she said, holding the phone between her ear and her shoulder while she typed. "Did you get those test results back in?"

She looked around for Yvette to make sure she wouldn't be caught on the phone. Yvette had been in an especially bad mood over the last few days, thanks to dealing with the recall. Not that she had to do any of the work herself. It was all coming across Tessa's desk, and all Yvette had to do was report the results to the people upstairs.

"Yeah, I've got them right here," Gregory said. "And I can tell you, this stuff definitely isn't made from oranges."

"Then what is it?"

Gregory started listing off a bunch of terms she didn't understand, but which certainly sounded like artificial chemicals. "Hold on," she said, interrupting him. "Give me the layperson's version."

"The compound is a rather harsh chemical herbicide. If this has been getting on your plants, even indirectly, it would definitely explain the problems you've been having."

Tessa sighed and rubbed at her eyes. It was what she'd expected, but now that she knew the truth, she wasn't sure what to do with the information. "Okay, thanks. I really appreciate this. Listen, can you email me a copy of those results."

"Sure thing."

She gave him her email address, then

thanked him again for all of his help. In between working on her reports for the rest of the day, she did some online research, looking up the kinds of chemicals Topher was using in his herbicide. While none of it was necessarily dangerous, it was still far from the all-natural, organic compounds that Tessa and the rest of the gardening community insisted on using. If Topher had his own private garden somewhere, where his chemicals wouldn't affect anyone else's crops, then that would be his own business. But it riled Tessa up to think of him spraying these poisons so close to her little garden, getting them into the soil and letting the wind carry them onto her tomatoes. She didn't use any kind of herbicide on her own plants. She did everything the old-fashioned way, pulling out weeds by hand and tending to her garden with loving care.

She wrapped up her work a bit early and ducked out of the office, not caring if Yvette would have anything to say about it. She'd worked enough extra hours over the past few days that she'd earned an early night out. When she got home, she opened a bottle of wine and sat in the seat by her window, looking out over the gardens. Samson was out there, tending to his herbs. So was Topher, measuring his tomatoes with a caliper and writing down the results on a notepad. She sipped her wine, watching him, then shook her head. Who *measured* their tomatoes like that? She just didn't understand him.

But she also didn't know what to do about him. The simplest thing would be to confront him, to tell him she knew he was using herbicides that were against the community rules. But he would just deny it, and even if she showed him the test results, he could easily claim that she had faked it. And what purpose would the confrontation serve? They would argue, he would attack her credibility, and it would do nothing other than creating a divide in the gardening community. Even if she got most of the other neighbors on her side, they technically couldn't ban Topher from doing what he wanted on his plot. He would just keep using whatever he wanted, and bragging about his amazing tomatoes. He'd go to the gardening show at the end of the season, win a blue ribbon, and show it off to everyone, making them all jealous of his skills and his success.

Tessa finished off her wine glass, a thought occurring to her. It was silly. Almost impractical. But it was also the best chance she had of getting back at Topher for what he'd done.

She grabbed her phone and called Samson. Even though he was right outside, she didn't want to go out to the garden and be seen by Topher. She felt a bit foolish for it, since it wasn't like he'd know she was conspiring against him.

But she felt like staying in her apartment, spying on the garden through the window, was the thing to do.

She watched Samson through the window as he jammed out to the music from his iPod, bobbing his head back and forth like an adorable dork while he tended his herbs. When his phone started ringing, he pulled out his ear buds, then patted his pockets until he found his phone.

"Hello?"

"Hey, babe," Tessa said. "I've got an idea."

Samson looked around, watching Topher. He lowered his voice as he spoke into the phone. "About the 'situation,' you mean?"

Tessa snickered at the way Samson was speaking in code. "Yes, dear, the 'situation.' Operation Show Topher Who's Boss. I think I know how to get back at him."

"I'm listening."

Out the window, she could see Samson eyeing Topher suspiciously. She shook her head, wondering if he was taking this too seriously. Or if she herself was.

"I think," she said, "that instead of trying to expose him, or stop him from using those herbicides, we need a different approach. It's not like we can really do anything about what he's doing."

"Yeah," Samson said. "I talked to Mrs. Mackenzie today. I didn't tell her I was asking about Samson, but I asked her what she thought the community could do if 'someone' was found to be violating the rules. She suggested a strongly worded letter. Or that the neighbors stop trading produce with the guilty party."

"All of which would be ultimately useless gestures." Tessa nodded, having come to the same conclusion as Samson.

"Topher would ignore a letter, and he doesn't trade with anyone anyway. He thinks his crops are too good for the likes of us."

"So what's your plan?"

Tessa smiled, pouring herself another glass of wine. She leaned back in her seat, studying Topher through the window and swirling her wine around in her glass. "Simple," she said. "You know how they say, 'fight fire with fire'?"

"You want to burn his plot down?"

"Ha! No." Tessa snorted. "But I think what we need to do is to take down Topher on his own terms."

She watched as he picked up a rather large squash, using his calipers to measure its width and height. He held it up with an admiring eye, nodding to himself.

"We're going to hit him where it hurts," Tessa said. "Right in the tomatoes."

Chapter Ten

They met that night at Terry's apartment. Terry served tea, while Tessa paced around the apartment, gesturing animatedly with her hands while she laid out her idea.

"Topher's completely focused on winning the gardening contest," she said. "He doesn't care about organic foods, healthy eating, getting in touch with the Earth, or any of that. He's in the gardening business for the prestige."

"Not a lot of prestige to be had for growing a tomato," Terry said, snorting.

"Not for most people." Tessa shrugged. "But in certain circles, it's a pretty big deal. Everything has its niche. Some people train for months to win video game tournaments. Other people try to get in the Guinness Book of World Records for the longest fingernails. To people in that niche, it's the most important thing in their world."

"And Topher's world," Samson said, while he cradled a steaming mug of tea in his hands, "is tomatoes."

"Bingo." Tessa drove a fist into her palm. "So if we want to pay Topher back for ruining our tomatoes, we need to beat him at his own game."

"So you want to poison his crops?" Terry asked, frowning. "Doesn't seem like the right thing to do. Especially when he isn't really hurting our tomatoes on purpose. He's a jerk, but he's not that mean."

"No," Tessa said, making a slashing motion with her hand. "We don't have to touch his tomatoes. We just need to grow better ones. And enter that gardening contest. And beat him."

Samson and Terry exchanged a look. Samson set down his tea and folded his hands. "Hon, I appreciate what you're trying to do here, but...your tomatoes are..."

She stared at him, a pout forming on her lips.

Samson cleared his throat and looked away. "Well, they're a bit shriveled, that's all. You won't be able to win a contest with them."

"And you can't just go to the store and buy a big tomato," Terry said. "I've never entered the contest myself, but I've been to a few. You're supposed to bring the whole plant, still on the vine. And to win, you have to have the biggest, ripest, most beautiful fruit of them all."

"And I can't see how we can grow a better tomato between now and the end of the season," Samson said, spreading his hands. "We've only got about six weeks, and it could take twice that long to grow something from scratch."

"And if you get caught trying to bring in something you didn't grow yourself,"

Terry added, "you could get disqualified. I know it might sound silly to get so worked up over a tomato, but like you said, people in that niche take this sort of thing real serious."

"Okay, I admit that the plan has some flaws," Tessa said. "But work with me here. Taking that blue ribbon away and making Topher walk away from that contest empty-handed is the best way we have to get back at him. We just need to find a way to make it happen."

"Okay," Samson said, "we'll make it happen. But how? We can't sabotage Topher's tomatoes, because that's cheating. And we can't grow our own tomatoes fast enough. So what does that leave us?"

Tessa drummed her fingers on the back of a chair, wracking her brain for the answer. It came to her in a flash. She snapped her fingers and pointed triumphantly into the air.

"We hire a ringer!"

* * *

One of the advantages to being part of a community of gardeners was that they all knew a lot of people, who all knew a lot of other people, who were all serious about gardening.

Over the next week, Tessa worked with Terry and Samson to network among everyone they knew, asking about who grew the best crops, the ripest tomatoes, and the finest produce in the county. Tessa did some online searches as well, searching various gardening blogs and forums. They found a few people that were already entered into the contest, which didn't do them any good. They needed someone that could represent their gardening community, someone they could sponsor in the competition so that Topher would know that they were the ones who beat him.

Eventually, Mrs. Mackenzie heard what they were up to and suggested they go speak to her nephew. "Conner's a wonderful gardener," she told Tessa over a glass of lemonade. "I taught him everything he knows, from when he was a little boy. That was when my husband was still alive, you understand. Conner used to come over to our house and help me tend our garden. Oh, it was so beautiful." A wistful look entered her eyes.

"Do you think he'd be interested in entering a contest?" Tessa asked.

"Why, I don't know," Mrs. Mackenzie said. "But it wouldn't hurt to ask. I'll give him a call and let him know you're interested in his tomatoes."

Tessa worried that such a phone call would sound weird, but it turned out that Conner was flattered. They made an arrangement to meet with him at his home out in the country. Tessa and Samson drove down there Saturday morning. Conner's house was surrounded by a beautiful flowering garden, and a wide field behind his home grew all sorts of fruits and vegetables. He greeted them as soon as they drove up and offered to take them on a tour of his fields.

"I never did think about entering a contest before," Conner said. He led them through the field, stopping here and there to check on some of his crops. He was dressed like a farmer in denim coveralls and a flannel shirt, with a wide-brimmed straw hat to protect him from the sun. "I sell most of what I grow. Well, what I don't eat, of course."

"Top prize is $250," Tessa said. "And a first place ribbon." She knew the cash prize was negligible compared to what some serious farmers and gardeners would spend on seeds, fertilizer, and other gardening supplies. Though she hoped it would be a nice incentive for Conner to join their cause.

"What would I have to do, exactly?" Conner asked. he stopped in front of a row of tomato plants. The crops were ripe and thriving. Tessa spotted a few tomatoes right away that might be good enough to enter into the contest.

"Well, there's a $10 entry fee," Tessa said. When Conner looked hesitant, she added, "But as your sponsors, we'd cover that, of course."

"We will?" Samson asked, frowning at her. She shot him a look. "Uhh, we will!"

"Plus we'd cover the cost of whatever you need to help get your crops ready for the show," Tessa said. "Extra fertilizer, that sort of thing."

"And, what?" Conner asked, frowning. "You'd want to split the prize money?"

"No, no!" Tessa shook her head and waved her hands in front of her. "You'd get to keep that. We're doing this for the prestige. The New Eden Apartments Gardening Community would just want our name listed as your sponsor. Get our name in the paper, along with yours. That sort of thing."

"Ahh." Conner rubbed his chin. "We'd be in the news, eh? Really?"

"Oh, definitely." Tessa kept a straight face, even though she wasn't actually sure about that part. But she figured the winner would be posted on some kind of news, *somewhere.*

"Well, it would be nice to get some acknowledgment for my work," Conner said. "Heck, might bring me some more business down at the farmer's market. I could hang up the picture." He held his hands up, framing the imagined photograph. "Conner Mackenzie's *Award Winning* Produce. I like the sound of that."

"So does that mean you'll do it?" Tessa smiled hopefully.

"Well, sure. Why not?" Conner grinned. "Err, you *did* say you'd be paying for it all, right?"

They worked out all of the

arrangements, and over the next few weeks, Tessa stopped by each weekend to check on Conner's tomatoes. She even snuck out at night to measure Topher's crops so she could compare them to Conner's and find out which were bigger. And she spent more money than she probably should have on high-end fertilizers to help give Conner's crops as much of a boost as they could get.

As the day of the gardening contest approached, she grew more and more nervous. She'd invested so much time and effort into this that she was starting to fear defeat. But she kept pressing forward. And every time she saw Topher out in the garden spraying his herbicide, it cemented her determination. She knew this was what she had to do.

Chapter Eleven

The night before the contest, Tessa and Samson had dinner together in her apartment. They talked for awhile over a bottle of wine, and eventually the topic of conversation came around to the gardening contest.

"Are you sure you're not becoming too obsessed with this?" Samson asked. He wore a look of concern.

"What? Me?" Tessa forced a laugh, shaking her head. "Look, I just want to make sure Topher gets what's coming to him, that's all. He ruined my tomato plants."

"So now you're going to ruin his chance to win the prize," Samson said.

Tessa frowned, giving her boyfriend an annoyed look. "Well, gee, when you say it like that, it almost sounds like I'm the bad guy."

Samson shrugged. He looked away, not meeting her eyes. "I'm not saying that, exactly."

"Then what, exactly?"

He sighed and chewed on his lip. "Look, all I'm saying is, you're putting an awful lot of effort into making sure Topher doesn't win a silly blue ribbon."

"And a cash prize."

"Yeah, and how much money have you spent in the last few weeks to keep him from winning that?"

Tessa looked away, digging her toe into the ground. "I'm not...sure. Exactly."

Samson gave her an impatient look. She refused to meet his eye. She hadn't *quite* spent as much as he thought on fertilizer. Just one jug of a really good brand that had cost her $124.95. Which wasn't *that* much. At least, that's what she kept telling herself.

"Maybe it's time to call it quits," Samson said.

"How can you say that?" Tessa planted her hands on her hips. "After what Topher did..."

"All he did was spray some herbicide on his weeds." Samson stepped forward and put his hands on her shoulders. "Honey, listen. I think I know what's really going on here."

"What's going on is—"

"Listen to me," Samson said. "You were feeling guilty about what happened to Terry when he got sick. You thought it was your fault, and when it turned out it wasn't, you were left without an outlet for your guilt. So you directed it at the only target that was available. And hey, I'm no real fan of Topher, either. But come on. Like it or not, he works hard all year long to prep for this contest. I don't think it's fair of us to steal that from him."

"I can't believe you're taking his side."

She pulled away, turning her back on him.

"I'm not taking anyone's side." Samson sighed. "Look, Tessa, you know I love you. But—"

"You do?" Tessa turned towards Samson, raising an eyebrow.

"Well, yeah." He shrugged and thrust his hands into his pockets.

Tessa pouted, crossing her arms and looking down at her feet. "Well, that's the first time you ever said it."

Samson came over to her and wrapped his arms around her. She held herself tense for a moment, then gave in and laid her head against his chest. "Maybe this wasn't the best time," Samson said. "But I mean it. I do love you."

"I love you too." Tessa closed her eyes, savoring the moment.

After a long silence, Samson said, "But I mean what I said. I think maybe you should give this up. Trying to get back at

Topher is turning you into a spiteful person. And that's not the Tessa I fell in love with."

She pulled away, shaking her head. "I think maybe you should go."

"Tessa..."

"Samson, please." She turned away, hugging her arms around herself. She was filled with too many conflicting emotions right now, and she couldn't sort them all out.

"All right," he said. "I guess I'll see you when you get back tomorrow."

She shot him a shocked look. "You're not coming?"

"No." His jaw was set in determination. "I'm sorry, babe. It just doesn't feel right. But...good luck."

"Gee, thanks."

Samson left, and Tessa found herself alone and confused. When this whole mess had started, everything had seemed so clear. Topher was the enemy, and the enemy had to be stopped. That was how these things worked.

But everything Samson had said was clashing with what she'd told herself she believed. Was she really just being spiteful? Was it possible that Topher wasn't such a bad guy after all?

She poured herself another glass of wine and sat by the window, looking out over the darkened gardens. In the faint light from her window, she could make out her own shriveled tomato plants. They'd withered away to almost nothing in the last few weeks. She hadn't really been tending to them at all.

She sipped at her wine, looking at her shriveled plants, and spent the rest of the night wrestling with the conflicting feelings churning inside of her.

Chapter Twelve

The morning of the gardening contest, Tessa went down to Terry's apartment and knocked on the door. He called for her to come in, and she found him huddled on his sofa, wearing his bathrobe and cradling a hot mug of tea in his hands.

"Oh, Tessa, dear," he said. "Is today the day? I've been a bit under the weather. I guess I just forgot."

"Is everything okay?" She looked him over with a concerned frown, fearing another trip to the hospital.

"Oh, nothing too serious." He forced a smile, though she could see the strain in his eyes. "Just my age catching up with me. Especially with all this heat we've been having lately."

"I don't want you to make yourself sick." She gave him a sympathetic smile and patted his shoulder. "You stay home and rest."

"All right. I hope you and Samson have a good time."

Tessa hesitated, not sure how to tell him that Samson wasn't coming. She decided to avoid the subject altogether. "I'm sure it's going to go great. I'll let you know when I get back."

She headed out alone and drove forty-five minutes to get to the location of the garden show. When she got there, she was surprised at how big of a spectacle it was. The event was being held at a farmer's market, and there were vendor stands lined up everywhere, selling everything from fresh produce to flowers to herbs to homemade arts and crafts.

There were also a number of events taking place, including a line of displays for people who had used cross-pollination to grow special types of plants that were resilient against pests. There was another event on floral arrangements, and one for "edible bouquets" made from fruits that had been carved to look like flowers. Then there was a children's event, where kids from kindergarten age to adolescence showed off their knowledge of photosynthesis and the life cycle of plants.

Tessa met Conner at the event for best produce, which was divided into different categories based on the type of fruit or vegetable on display. There were about a dozen entrants with tomato plants, each of them growing some of the biggest, plumpest, most ripe fruits Tessa had ever seen. They were all working on arranging their displays, spritzing water on the plants to keep them fresh, and doing last-minute pruning to make sure everything looked its best.

Tessa helped Conner set up his

display, along with a poster she'd made at home declaring the New Eden Apartments Gardening Community as Conner's sponsors. Though technically she was the only member of the community who had done any sponsoring.

She did her best not to look directly at Topher while she was setting up, but he spotted her and came over to talk to her. "Tessa?" he asked. "I didn't know you were going to be here."

He eyed Conner's tomato plant critically, sizing up the competition.

"Well, you always talked about it so much," Tessa said. "I figured I should come by sometime."

"But this isn't one of yours," he said, gesturing to the plant.

"Well, no."

He studied the poster, frowning. "You're...sponsoring someone? That...that's weird." He scratched the back of his head. "Why not grow your own? You grow tomatoes, don't you?"

"Well, my crop didn't come in very well this year," she said, crossing her arms. "Thanks to you."

"Thanks to me?" He got a confused look on his face. "What did I do?"

"That herbicide you've been spraying?" She stared him down, finally ready for the confrontation that had been weeks in coming. "The wind's been picking it up and spraying it onto my plants. My poor tomatoes withered away to almost nothing!" She threw her arms up in the air, her voice raising near the end of her tirade.

"Oh." Topher chewed on his lip. "Well, why didn't you tell me?"

Tessa blinked, lowering her arms. "What?"

"Why didn't you tell me my spray was getting on your crops?" He gave her a confused look, sympathy showing in his eyes. "I could have put down tarps or something to contain it. I didn't know."

"But...but you..." Tessa shook her head, unable to form a coherent thought.

"We're all a community, aren't we?" He shrugged, keeping his head down. "I know you don't like me much, or whatever, but I would've done something about it. If you'd told me."

"I..." Tessa stared at him, mute. "I...I guess I didn't think about it."

"Whatever." He shrugged and turned away. "Sorry, I guess. I'll be more careful next time."

He headed back to his own plants, checking over them one last time before the judging.

Tessa sat down on the stool by Conner's display. She felt dizzy. It slowly started to sink in. All these weeks, planning Topher's downfall...and she had never even tried just *talking* to him. Like a reasonable, responsible adult would have done.

"I am *such* an ass," she whispered,

lowering her head into her hands.

Her head was still spinning when the judges started coming around. She looked up at them, watching the group move from one display to another. They made notes and took measurements, checking each plant's height, weighing the tomatoes, and making other objective assessments. The winner would be judged based on the highest score in several categories, including size, color, and several other measurements. The judges made their way down the line, taking a few minutes at each display. By the time they got to Topher's display, Tessa was on the verge of having a panic attack.

"Oh no, oh no, oh no." She got up and started pacing back and forth in front of Conner's display, wringing her hands.

"Hey, don't be so nervous," Conner said. "It ain't the end of the world if we lose."

She ignored him. All she could think

about was how she was such a horrible person for going through so much effort to crush Topher's ambitions, when he hadn't done anything wrong at all. She hadn't even *talked* to him about her concerns. She had always thought Topher was an odd fellow, and a bit standoffish, but she should have at least given him a chance. Treated him like a human being.

The judges were only one table away. She looked between them and Conner's display, trying to think. She thought about smashing the tomato, ripping the vine up by its roots, or flipping the table over. Anything to keep from winning. But then she saw the eager smile on Conner's face. She'd dragged him into this, and it wouldn't be fair for her to ruin things for him.

She was stuck. There was nothing she could do but stand there and wait.

She stood there wringing her hands as the judges walked over to their table.

She felt like she was going to throw up. She never wanted to look at another stupid tomato again in her entire life.

She forced a smile as the judges greeted them. The judges were quiet as they made their assessments. Then they thanked Tessa and Conner, before moving on. Tessa sat back down, burying her face in her hands, and silently praying for this to all be over soon.

It felt like forever before the judges came over to make their announcements. Tessa sat on the edge of her seat. She saw Topher leaning forward nervously. He looked as anxious about winning as Tessa was, though for completely different reasons.

"And first prize," one of the judges said, "for best tomato is...Topher Caldwell!"

Tessa heaved a sigh of relief. Conner made a frustrated gesture with his hand and said, "Aww, well. Good show, anyway, right?"

Conner ended up taking third place and winning a yellow ribbon. He held it up with pride and beamed as his picture was taken. Tessa congratulated him, then headed over to Topher's table.

"Hey, Topher."

He looked up at her, then ducked his head back down, fiddling with the leaves of his plant. "Hi."

"I just wanted to congratulate you. You deserved this."

A shy smile showed on his face, though he didn't quite make eye contact. "Thanks. I had a bigger one last year." He patted his tomato lovingly, then shrugged.

She touched his arm and smiled. "Well, congratulations. I'm happy for you."

She turned away, feeling waves of relief wash over her. She'd made a fool of herself, dragged people into her crazy scheme, and nearly ruined the biggest day of Topher's year. But at least, she told herself, things had worked out in the end.

Except, she realized, for one last problem. She still had to go home and apologize to Samson.

Chapter Thirteen

When Tessa got home, she headed for Samson's apartment and knocked on the door. She hadn't knocked for months, but somehow, it felt like she needed to this time.

There was no answer. She knocked again, and waited. When there was still no answer, she let herself in. Samson wasn't home. Though when she looked outside she saw him out in the garden, laughing with some of the neighbors as he passed around mugs of his herbal tea.

She stood in his apartment, wringing her hands. She knew she needed to go out there and talk to him, but she didn't know what to say. "I'm sorry" was the obvious thing, but it didn't seem like enough. Looking back on her behavior over the last few weeks, she knew she'd been a complete idiot. And now that it was time to face up to it, she realized she had no idea how to do it.

She was pacing around his apartment when she saw him look her way through the window. He gave her a wave, and she paused in her pacing, waving back. He set down his mug of tea on a bench outside and entered the apartment through the back door.

"Hey," he said, a small smile touching his lips. "How did the show go?"

"We lost." She shrugged.

"Ahh." He stuck his hands in his pockets, looking down at his feet.

"Listen," she said. She chewed on her lip, trying to figure out what to say.

He waited for a moment, then smiled and her and said, "Let me guess. You realized you were being kind of an ass, figured out how wrong that was, and now you're feeling guilty?"

"See, now that's not fair!" She threw

her arms out to either side. "You don't get to come in here, and be all...all..."

"Right?" he asked, a smug grin on his face.

"Well...yeah." She pouted, looking up at him.

"Tessa, it's okay." He stepped forward and slipped his arms around her waist. "I was just as much of an ass as you were. I just figured it out a little bit sooner."

"So, we're a couple of asses, then. Is that what you're saying?"

He shrugged. "Well, we do seem to have a track record of making bad decisions together."

She laughed and laid her head against his chest. "Can we do anything right?"

"We did one thing right."

He touched his fingers under her chin to tilt her face up towards him. She smiled, fighting back tears. "You're going to be a total dork," she said, giggling, "and say 'the one thing we did right is us.'"

He laughed and rolled his eyes. "Well, way to take away my romantic steam!"

They held each other close and laughed, then they kissed, and Tessa's worries and tensions started to melt away. She looked up at Samson, smiling, and thinking how lucky she was to have someone who was so understanding, and so willing to put up with her craziness.

"I love you," she said.

"And I love you."

"Just promise me one thing?"

"Anything." He smiled and stroked her hair.

"Next time I come up with some crazy scheme," she said, "just pour me a glass of wine, lock me in my room, and tell me to forget all about it."

He laughed and hugged her tight. "Tessa my dear, you've got yourself a deal."

THE END

TESSA'S SUMMER

Tessa's Autumn

Chapter One

She pulled over a small wheelbarrow and laid down a clean tarp in it, then pulled several of the largest, ripest watermelons off the vine and loaded them into it. She set one aside for herself, then started making the rounds of her neighbors in the small apartment complex, offering each of them first pick.

"Mrs. Mackenzie," she said, greeting her elderly neighbor. "The watermelons are finally ready. I wanted to give you first pick."

"Oh, I couldn't take a whole one just for myself," Mrs. Mackenzie said. She pulled off her gardening gloves and looked over the selection. "My, my, but these are lovely. I'll tell you what, you bring one of those over later this afternoon, and bring that boyfriend of yours along. We'll share."

"Sounds wonderful," Tessa said, grinning wide. "We'll be along after we get done out here."

She stopped to chat with a few other neighbors, each of whom were tending to their own gardens in the little community gardening patch that stood between two apartment buildings. With the fall rapidly approaching, squash and pumpkins were becoming some of the most common sights in the gardens. Tessa even had a little patch of pumpkins in her own plot, though it would be a few weeks yet before they were ripe. She was hoping to have them ready in time for Halloween. There were a lot of families with small children in the apartment complex, and they were always eager to go picking pumpkins to carve into Jack O' Lanterns.

She gave one of the biggest watermelons to Topher, her odd neighbor who tended to keep to himself a lot. "I picked this one out just for you," she said, lifting the watermelon out and handing it to him.

"Wow, thanks," he said, taking it into his arms. "Damn, this puppy is huge. Coloring's not the best for display, of course. I could give you some pointers."

"I'm just worried about it tasting good," Tessa said, forcing a smile. She and Topher had never quite been friends, and the way he sometimes seemed to look down on other people's crops for not being as perfect as his made him a hard person to like. But she'd come to understand him a bit better over the summer, and she knew his heart was in the right place, even if he was too socially awkward to realize when he was being rude. The watermelon was a bit of a peace offering, her way of letting him know that she had never intended to treat him as an outcast. It was the least she could do, after the way she'd tried to crash his gardening contest a few months ago.

After she'd delivered the last of her watermelons, since she already had the wheelbarrow out, Tessa made another trip around the gardens to collect any weeds and other refuse that needed to go out to the compost pile. The gardeners all tried to work together to keep everything organic and reduce waste, and the compost was useful for making all-natural fertilizer. She rolled the wheelbarrow around the back of the building and headed for the fenced-off area where they kept the community compost heap.

While she was standing behind the

fence, dumping everything out of the wheelbarrow, she heard a voice call out, "Whew! What is that smell?"

"Oh, they keep a compost pile back here. Part of the gardening group."

Tessa peeked out from behind the fence to see who it was. She saw Hank, her landlord, walking with another man, who was wearing a suit and holding a clipboard. She frowned, wondering what was going on.

"Do they have a permit for that?" the man in the suit asked. "Or is this something the complex has to deal with?"

"I'm not real clear on the laws around this sort of thing," Hank said. "But from what I understand, no permits are needed for something as small as this. Only for large-scale industrial compost sites."

"So they only maintain it with your permission?" The man in the suit made some notes on his clipboard.

"That's right."

"Do you have that in writing somewhere?"

"No, nothing like that," Hank said. "They just asked if they could do it, same with the gardens. I sent a letter out to all the tenants letting them know about the request, and nobody protested it, so I told them they could go ahead and do it"

Tessa crouched down lower by the edge of the fence, trying to better hear what the men were talking about. She had never heard Hank discussing the gardens with anyone before, and she wasn't sure what was going on.

"If it's not in writing," the man in the suit said, "then we won't have to worry about shutting it down." He nodded to himself as he wrote on his clipboard.

Tessa gasped, covering her mouth with her hand. Hank was planning to shut down the gardens?

"How much space are we talking about in the garden area itself?" the man asked as he and Hank started walking again.

"Around thirty-two hundred square feet," Hank said. "The area between the buildings is bigger than that, but I said they needed to keep the gardens a reasonable distance from the building walls."

"Thirty-two hundred? Hmm. That could work. Mid-rise building, twelve to sixteen units, four per floor. Maybe more than that if we extend past this tree line. How far back there does the property extend?" He gestured towards the patch of woods that surrounded the apartment complex.

They moved too far away after that for Tessa to make out the rest of what they were saying, but she'd heard enough. Hank was planning on shutting down the gardens to make room for another apartment building. The very idea made her skin crawl. Not only would it destroy the gardening community and the freedom they all shared, but it would also take away the outdoor lifestyle and wide open, natural feel that had always been such a big part of the apartment complex's charm. Squeezing another building in where the gardens were now would be like turning the complex into a tightly packed urban area, completely ruining the entire spirit of the place.

She left the wheelbarrow where it was and hurried back to the gardens to find her boyfriend, Samson. She needed to tell him what was going on, and they needed to find out if there was any way they could put a stop to it.

Chapter Two

Tessa searched the gardens for Samson, but he wasn't by his little patch where he grew mostly herbs and spices. She asked around, and found he had already gone to Mrs. Mackenzie's apartment to help her prepare dinner. When she got to the apartment, she found him inside, slicing up the watermelon along with some other fruit to make a fruit salad.

"Come on in, dear," Mrs. Mackenzie said when she opened the door. "I've got just the job for you. Come give me a hand in the kitchen."

Tessa followed her into the kitchen, but her mind was on anything but dinner. "Something's wrong," she said.

"I don't know, but..."

"Tessa?" Samson asked, giving her a concerned look. "What's the matter?"

"I was over by the compost heap," Tessa explained, "and I saw Hank out there with some strange man."

"Hank the landlord?"

"Yeah. They were talking, and, well..."

Samson frowned. He put his hands on her arms, holding her steady. "Tessa, what is it? Did something happen?"

"I think they're planning to close down the gardens."

"Oh my," Mrs. Mackenzie said, putting a hand to her chest. "Tessa dear, are you sure?"

"Well, I think so."

Samson studied her face, wearing a contemplative frown. "Tessa, you tend to have an overactive imagination. Why don't you sit down and tell us what happened?"

Tessa took a seat at the kitchen table. Mrs. Mackenzie poured her a glass of lemonade. She explained everything she had overheard outside, including the part about building another apartment building where the gardens now stood.

"But that doesn't make sense," Mrs. Mackenzie said. "We've had our gardens there for years. Can they just shut them down?"

"Legally, they probably can," Samson said. "We don't own the land the garden is on. And it's not even part of our apartment leases. Hank's always been cool about it, though. Why would he change his mind now?"

"I don't think it's Hank," Tessa said. "It sounded more like this other man was the one planning the changes."

"What do you think is going on, then?" Samson asked. He reached up to straighten his ponytail, a nervous habit Tessa had noticed he had whenever he had a lot on his mind. "Is Hank selling the property?"

"Maybe?" Tessa shrugged. "I don't

really know. Don't we have any say in it?"

"Probably not," Samson said. "Our leases are with the apartment complex itself, so if the complex changes ownership, our leases get carried over to the new owner, who can more or less do whatever he wants, I would imagine."

"That's nonsense," Mrs. Mackenzie said, smacking a hand on the table and sitting up straighter. "I've got a lease, in writing. They can't change that."

"No, they can't," Samson said. "But they can wait until your lease expires and change the renewal terms any way they please. Though they wouldn't even need to change the terms to get rid of the gardens, since they aren't in the lease as it is."

"What are we going to do? We need to keep this garden going. It's so much more than just a plot of dirt now." Tessa said. She wrung her hands, wracking her mind for a solution. She loved her garden, and the community she was a part of. She had met Samson, the man she loved, in that garden.

It was more than just her hobby. It was where she came at the end of each day to relax, to commune with nature, and to remind herself of the deep satisfaction that came with putting your hands into the dirt and growing something from a seed into a flourishing plant that nourished people's lives. The garden had created strong bonds that most apartment dwellers didn't have the chance for.

"The first thing I think we should do," Samson said, "is not jump to any conclusions. You know how that usually goes for us."

"Yeah...I guess you're right." Tessa smiled in agreement. She had a bad habit of getting the wrong idea about something and acting on it, without actually making sure that things were the way she thought they were.

"We should go talk to Hank," Mrs. Mackenzie said, smacking a fist into her palm. "Ask him straight out what's going on. If he's planning on selling the complex, he has an obligation to tell us."

"I'll talk to a few other tenants," Samson said. "Terry Jones, a couple of the others who have been here awhile. Maybe we can go down on Saturday when it's time to pay the rent. If all of us show up together, as a show of the community spirit, he'll have to talk to us."

"That sounds like a good idea," Tessa said. She smiled up at Samson. "I should come to you with my problems more often. You're always the sensible one."

"But you're the brave one," he said, caressing her cheek. "You're always the one who wants to stand up and fight for what you believe in."

Tessa knew that he was right. She would always stand up for what she believed in. And she believed in this garden community. More than anything else she'd ever had in her life.

Chapter Three

Getting through the rest of the week was difficult. Tessa founds herself distracted at work, and one day she accidentally submitted two reports to the wrong offices, resulting in some major confusion before she got things sorted out and got everything submitted where it needed to go. She couldn't even concentrate on her gardening when she got home each night. Every time she looked around the various plots where each of her neighbors tended their gardens, all she could do was picture it all being bulldozed to make room for another apartment building that would crowd out the entire block.

Word about the developer and his plans spread quickly throughout the community. On the second day after she'd overheard the plans, Tessa was approached by half a dozen people, asking her if it was true. Even Topher came over to ask her what she had overheard.

"I heard we might all be getting evicted," Topher said. "Is that true?"

"Where did you hear that?" Tessa frowned, wondering if the story was being exaggerated. Rumors had a way of getting blown out of proportion when they were told and retold. She didn't want anyone in the community to start panicking. Usually, that was her job.

"Mark told me that Susan told him that Samson told her that we were all getting kicked out," Topher said. He ran a hand nervously through his hair. "Something about violating local laws by not having things up to code. Like you'd need permits or something."

"I don't think that's true." Tessa tapped a finger to her lips. She didn't really know much about the law in this regard, but she doubted that it would be illegal to grow vegetables in your own backyard. "I don't think anyone is getting kicked out. But if they want to shut down the gardens, I'm not sure what we can do about it, since we don't own the property."

"This sucks," Topher said, stalking off and grumbling to himself. He headed back to his garden, which he had surrounded with a low wall of tarps in an effort to keep the wind from carrying his pesticides out onto the rest of the gardens. He started pruning some of his plants, his movements filled with nervous energy. Tessa knew exactly how he must have felt. She was filled with nerves as well, and it was hard for her to sit still. The Saturday intervention couldn't get here soon enough.

When Saturday morning finally came, Tessa wrote out her rent check and headed down to the office. She found

Samson and a few others already waiting there for her. Samson had dressed up for the occasion; he usually wore hand-woven clothes and sandals, or t-shirts with the names of local indie bands. Today he had put on tan slacks and a polo shirt, making him look almost respectable.

"Trying to make a good impression?" Tessa asked, smirking at him.

"I've learned the hard way that people don't tend to take you seriously when you dress like a hipster hippie." A wry grin spread on his face. "They tend to dismiss you as the kind of person who has a different cause every day of the week, from saving the whales to the rain forests to stopping global warming."

"But you actually *do* fight for all of those things," Tessa said.

"I know." Samson shrugged. "But if I distance myself from that image, Hank is more likely to take me seriously."

"So you're going to be our voice for

this?"

"No, actually." He scratched the back of his head. "We were talking about that, and everyone thinks you should be."

"Me?" Tessa's eyes widened. "Why?"

"Well, you're the one who brought it to everyone's attention. And everyone likes you and respects you."

"They do?" Tessa asked, lowering her voice. She looked around, wondering what people had been saying about her when she wasn't around. Though it seemed they were all saying *good* things. It was just that she had never thought of herself as that great of a person. She tried to do what she thought was right, sure, but that was a long way from being some kind of leader.

"Trust me." Samson took her by her shoulders and steered her towards the office door. "Now, let's march in there and tell Hank that we want to know what's going on."

He nudged her forward, and the rest

of the crowd started following along. Nearly a dozen people had shown up, far more than Tessa was expecting. Though it made her feel good to know that so many people cared about the community. They probably could have gotten even more than this if they'd tried hard enough.

They walked into the office and found Julie, the office assistant, sitting behind the front desk. She looked up at them, her eyes widening when she saw how many people there were. "Hi. Is everyone here with rent checks?"

Tessa glanced at the group behind her. Samson gave her an encouraging smile and nudged her forward. "Yes," she said, smiling at Julie. "Well, no. Sort of."

"Sort of?" Julie frowned.

"Well, I mean, I am here to pay the rent." She placed her check on the desk. "But I...we...need to speak to Hank. Please."

Julie looked at the size of the group again, twisting her pen between her fingers. "Can I ask what this is about?"

Tessa took a deep breath. "Tell him we want to ask him if he's really selling the complex."

Julie's eyebrows shot up and her face went a bit pale. "Oh. That. Right. Okay. Hold on one second."

She got up and headed into the back office. A few moments later, she returned with Hank by her side. Julie sat down at her desk and started writing out a receipt for Tessa's rent check, keeping her head down. Hank put his hands on his hips and looked over the group.

"Well," Hank said. "I'm not sure what you people have all been told, or where you heard it, but—"

"I saw you talking with that man the other day," Tessa said. "Over by the compost heap. He was talking about tearing down the gardens and putting up another apartment building there."

Hank sighed, running a hand through his balding red hair. "Is that so?"

"Yes." Tessa stood up a bit straighter. "And..." She glanced back at Samson. He gave her a supportive smile and nodded for her to continue. She turned back to Hank and said, "And frankly, Hank, those of us who have lived here for years think we deserve some kind of answer about this. Are you really selling the complex?"

Hank rubbed a hand over his bearded chin. "I was going to call a community meeting about this in a week or two," he said.

"So it's true." Tessa felt the energy drain out of her body.

Multiple people started talking at once. Hank held up his hands to silence them. "Now, nothing is settled yet. I've been in talks with a developer who is planning on buying up several apartment complexes in this area. Our complex, Stonebridge Apartments down the road, Shady Palms across the way. A few others. You all know there's been a lot of new business expansion in this area lately. New shopping centers and office complexes have been cropping up. Heck, we got *two* new Walmarts in the last five years."

"What does that have to do with anything?" Tessa asked.

"Well, when an area has this much growth, there's a lot of room for an expanding residential district. But it's not like there's a lot of undeveloped land in the area. Not in any good locations, anyway. So this developer is considering buying up some of the existing residential properties and expanding them. Building new structures in the unused parts of the existing land."

"Like building over our gardens," Mrs. Mackenzie said, raising her chin and looking down her nose at Hank.

"That would be up to him," Hank said. "Now, you all know I don't mind letting you have that space to use for your gardens. I've been fine with it. But if Mr. Donaldson buys the property, then he can do with it as he pleases, and that's that."

"So you'd just sell us out?" Tessa asked, frowning.

"Don't make it like that." Hank sighed. "Look, the economy has been down for years, you all know that. I've been trying my best not to raise the rent above the rate of inflation each year, but I'm struggling. I don't have the money or the resources to do what it would take to improve things around here. I keep up with maintenance and all that, but these apartments are old. A lot of them really need to be gutted and revamped. New kitchens, modern appliances, and more. A few years ago I planned to try to fix up any of the apartments where there's turnover. When someone moves out, get the place fixed up and modernized, so that when a new tenant comes in the apartment is worth more and can go for a higher rent. It's what this place needs in order to survive, but I can't afford to make the upgrades."

"Some people would rather have reasonable rent than upgrades. So you're going to toss us aside in order to make more money?" Tessa said, crossing her arms.

"Now, that's not fair." Hank cast a stern look across the entire group. "It's either this, or I risk going bankrupt. Now, I haven't made a final decision yet. But Mr. Donaldson has made me an offer, and if I take it, then he would become your new landlord. As I understand it, he plans to hire an office manager for each of the complexes he buys, so whoever that is, that's who you'd have to talk to. Any decision about what happens to the gardens is, frankly, out of my hands." He spread his hands to either side.

Tessa looked back to Samson. He had

a stern set to his jaw, and his lips were pressed together in a thin line. He met her eyes, then gave a small shake of his head.

Tessa looked back at Hank, fighting off tears. "So that's it then?"

"I'm sorry," Hank said. "I really am. I know how much your gardens mean to you. But I've got to make the best decision for me, here. Now, you can always talk to Mr. Donaldson once he takes over. Try to convince him not to tear down the gardens. But once he owns the property, that becomes his call. And...frankly, I'm sorry, but I can't risk going bankrupt here just to save some pumpkin patches and whatnot."

There was some grumbling among the gathered tenants, but no one seemed to have anything else to say. Hank raised his hands and said, "Now, if that's all, please, everyone drop off your rent checks and head on home."

The tenants formed a disorganized

line in front of Julie's desk, dropping off their rent checks one at a time. As they filed outside, a few of them went home, while others lingered in front of the office in small groups, talking about what had happened.

Tessa stood with Samson and a couple of others. She crossed her arms and lowered her head, feeling defeated. "That felt like a complete waste of time."

"Not necessarily," Samson said.

"What do you mean?"

"Well, we know some things we didn't know before." Samson raised a hand and started ticking off points on his fingers. "One, Hank's having financial troubles. Maybe if we found another way for him to avoid bankruptcy, we could convince him not to sell. Two, Donaldson is planning to buy a bunch of other properties in the area. Maybe if we could convince some of the others not to sell, he'd back out of the whole project."

"I still think maybe there's a legal

angle we can pursue." Tessa suggested. "Like, exercising our rights to use the land since we've been working it for so long."

"Maybe." Samson shrugged. "It's worth looking into. But at least now we know for sure what's happening, and why. All we need to do now is figure out a plan."

Tessa looked over at the gardens, nestled between the buildings. "Yeah. And we've only got about a month to come up with one."

Chapter Four

Sunday afternoon, Tessa sat together with Samson, Mrs. Mackenzie, and Terry Jones, discussing the options they had available to them. They had all agreed that moving out and finding another place to live had to be the last resort.

For one thing, since they saw each other out in the garden almost every day, they had become good friends, and it wasn't likely that they would all end up at the same apartment complex together again if they all ended up moving. For another thing, there wasn't much chance of finding another apartment complex in the area that would let the tenants build a community garden patch. So the best option that they had was to find a way to keep their current home from being changed.

"Okay," Tessa said, holding up a notepad where she'd listed the ideas she'd come up with so far. "I did some research online last night, looking into the laws and such, trying to figure out what kind of options we have. I kind of just listed them in whatever order they came to me." She looked over her list, taking a deep breath, then starting with the first item on the list. "First, we could try to do a fundraiser. Either raise enough money to buy part of the land ourselves, or to use it to keep the complex from going bankrupt so we could keep living here."

"That doesn't seem too practical," Terry said, rubbing his chin. A patch of gray stubble covered his face, marking the long years he'd lived through. "I mean, how much money would we be talking about here?"

"Yeah, that's the problem," Tessa said, her lips twisted in a grimace. "I don't know what Mr. Donaldson is offering Hank, but I researched some similar apartment complexes online. They tend to sell for anywhere from three hundred thousand to over a million dollars."

"We could never raise that kind of money," Mrs. Mackenzie said, frowning and shaking her head. "If I had that much money, I'd buy a condo down in Florida!"

"Yeah, I didn't think that was the best idea." Tessa crossed it off her list. "Okay, we can try to block the construction legally. Though usually they only use that tactic for historic sites and landmarks, that sort of thing."

"Our garden isn't exactly a landmark," Samson said, crossing his arms. "I mean, we all love it, but to anyone who doesn't live here, it's nothing more than a patch of dirt."

"Right." Tessa crossed the second

option off her list. "Okay, this one is a bit better. We rally the tenants together for a protest. Not just here, but at all the other complexes for sale."

"What would they care about our gardens?" Terry asked, harrumphing. "I doubt we could even get every tenant who lives here to join us. Only about half the tenants have plots in the garden patch, and there's a few of those that aren't as passionate about it as the rest of us. Gathering the few dozen of us who really need this...I just don't see it being enough."

"Well, it doesn't have to just be about the garden," Tessa said, gesturing with her pen. "See, we can pitch this as being a movement against urban development. Remember when they did that big construction project in Marlton a few years back? Taking out the traffic circle and putting in the overpass?"

"What about it?" Samson asked.

"Well, there was a lot of protest at the

time. People were saying that the overpass would be an eyesore in the middle of the town, and it would be ruining the small town feeling of the neighborhood. We might be able to get some people rallied about that idea."

"Yeah, but it didn't work in Marlton, right? Samson asked. "I mean, the overpass got built."

Tessa sunk back into her seat a bit. "Well, maybe this time it would work out better."

Mrs. Mackenzie patted the back of Tessa's hand. "It sounds like a good idea, dear, but aren't the people in those other complexes mostly young folks with families? Young people these days don't seem to care as much about community and the heart of a small town. They see all this development as a good thing. More stores for them to go shopping in. More jobs for them to support their families. And I respect that, I do. But I'm retired, and I can only support myself on my retirement savings and my social security." She shook her head, a sad look in her eyes. "If they raise the rent here like Hank said they might, I won't be able to afford to stay any longer."

"And I don't want to wind up in one of those old folk's apartment homes," Terry said, crossing his arms. "People go there to die. I like it here because in those gardens, I'm surrounded by life."

Tessa smiled warmly at Terry. She knew he had spent a long part of his life in prison. He probably craved the outdoors and the sunshine more than most people, after spending so many years behind cold stone walls and iron bars.

"All right," Tessa said, letting out a long sigh. She crossed another item off her list. "What about meeting with Mr. Donaldson ourselves? Letting him know our concerns as a community."

"Now that's not a bad idea," Samson said. "But do you think we can get him to listen to us?"

"Well, we can approach it a few different ways." Tessa consulted her notes, tapping her pen against her lips. "We could go to him with a list of demands. Insist that he let us keep the gardens."

"Or else what?" Terry asked. "We threaten not to pay our rent? Even if he doesn't raise the rent on us, that's not much of a threat. He'd be able to evict us, then redo the apartments the way he wants and get a bunch of new tenants. It's not like he'll have trouble filling the apartments. This whole area is overpopulated. There's always people looking for a place to live. And making demands to the person with the power usually backfires."

"And he doesn't even have to offer us lease renewals," Samson added. "When each of our leases come up, he has the legal option, as long as he gives us like sixty days notice or something like that, to just let us know he's not renewing the leases. Or he could offer us new leases at prices he knows we can't afford."

"Okay, so we don't make demands," Tessa said. "We reason with him."

"People like that only listen to money," Terry said.

"Okay, so..." Tessa paused, a thought occurring to her. She looked off into the distance, her eyes unfocused as she focused on her internal thoughts, trying to work out the idea that she had forming.

"Tessa?" Samson asked. He reached across the table and took her hand.

"Money," Tessa said.

"Yeah, that's what I said," Terry said.

"No, I mean, that's how we have to handle this."

"We already said a fundraiser wouldn't work, dear," Mrs. Mackenzie said.

"No, we don't need to raise money." She raised her pen in the air triumphantly. "We need to make sure that the apartments are more profitable now than they would be after the renovations. The developer said he could fit a small building in the space we have available. Enough room for twelve or sixteen units. That's, what, $9600 to $12,000 per month total income, depending on how much he charges for rent on the new building."

"Minus all the costs associated with it," Samson said. "I did a little research. He might need to drop eighty to a hundred grand or more on construction and development before he even has any new apartments to rent."

"Not to mention increases in property taxes," Tessa added. "If they add another building, property taxes for the complex go up."

"I don't see where you're going with this, dear," Mrs. Mackenzie said.

"I need to do some more research," Tessa said. She got up from the chair and headed for the door. "We'll meet back here tomorrow night."

"Tessa," Samson asked, "can you at least tell us what you're thinking?"

She paused at the door and flashed him a smile. "Just wait. I want to make sure I have this right, but if I do, it's going to be perfect."

Chapter Five

Tessa spent the rest of the night doing some research online. There were a few avenues she wanted to explore, though she ran into some dead ends fairly early on.

The community garden was fairly small, only about thirty-two hundred square feet total. That was divided up into almost three dozen small garden patches of a hundred square feet each. Not nearly big enough to do major farming—and thus, not anywhere near enough to potentially get the complex a tax break for farmers. The gardeners didn't even sell the vegetables they grew on their little patches of dirt. Like Tessa, they tended to share the goods among the community, though a few people like Topher grew vegetables they brought down to gardening shows to win prizes. The state law only offered tax breaks to farmers with at least five acres. And Tessa couldn't find any laws that applied specifically to small gardening communities like theirs.

Eventually, though, she found some things in her research that would make for good arguments from the perspective of how much money the property was worth. A well-maintained garden could do a lot for property value, something she was sure Hank hadn't taken into consideration when Mr. Donaldson made him an offer. It was likely that if the property was formally appraised, the presence of the gardens would make a big difference in the appraised price.

Another point she found was the savings in maintenance. The gardens were maintained entirely at the expense of the tenants. Each person paid for their own seeds, fertilizer, and other gardening supplies. And the thirty-two hundred square feet of space they maintained the garden in was land that Hank had never had to pay his maintenance crew to work on. This meant that the presence of the garden saved him money every year, taking a big chunk out of the price Hank had to pay for landscaping throughout the rest of the complex.

Added together with the cost of constructing and maintaining the new building, the increase in property taxes that would result from the expansion, and the loss in rent the complex would suffer if all of the gardeners decided to move out, and the numbers were pretty clear. The only way that Mr. Donaldson could make a profit on his planned purchase and expansion of the property would be to low-ball Hank on the price he had offered. If Donaldson paid what the property was really worth, at least by

Tessa's estimation, he'd end up taking a major loss. And somehow Tessa had the feeling that Hank had no idea what the real value of his property was. He couldn't have, or else he never would have agreed to the deal.

She spent some time typing up everything she had learned, formatting it the same way she would the reports she submitted at her office. Like Samson had said the day before, appearance really did matter. Hank would never take her seriously if she went to him with a bunch of notes scrawled on a yellow legal pad. But if she could write up a report that would show him, clearly in black and white on the page, how much his property was really worth, then she might just be able to convince him not to sell.

Or, on the other hand, she might be able to convince Mr. Donaldson that if he did buy the property, the value of the gardens was worth more to him than the value of adding another building to the complex. It would all be a matter of how she presented her case.

Chapter Six

The next day, Tessa brought her report to Samson, Terry, and Mrs. Mackenzie. The two elderly residents only gave it a cursory glance, before saying that the numbers were too confusing. But Samson sat and read the report over carefully, stopping to ask her a few questions here and there as he read.

When he finished reading, he said, "This is pretty good work, Tessa. If I were Hank and I read this, I'd be pretty mad about the developer trying to rip me off. And if Donaldson reads it, assuming he's willing to listen, he might decide that buying the complex is too big of a financial risk. Either way, we might manage to get one or both of them on our side."

"There's just one problem," Terry said. "You heard what Hank said the other day. He's on the verge of going bankrupt. What if he's desperate enough to take the lower offer from Donaldson?"

"Hank has every right to sell if he wants to," Tessa said. She paced around the apartment, sorting out her thoughts as she went. "But he also deserves to be paid what the place is worth. Frankly, I think our best bet here is if Donaldson does buy the complex, but decides to let us keep the gardens. Or maybe we can find another developer to make Hank an offer. Someone who would be willing to buy the place as-is without any plans for putting up another building."

"And this report," Samson said, holding up the pages, "actually makes a pretty good case for the complex being a good investment. We sell our prospective developer on the idea that having the gardens raises the value of the property and the appeal to new tenants, giving people added incentive to want to move in here. And the reduced landscaping costs is a good angle. I don't know what Hank spends on landscaping here, but it's got to be a fraction of what it would be if we weren't maintaining the gardens free of charge. It sounds to me like a win-win situation."

"But what's to stop a new owner from raising the rent?" Terry asked. "I mean, if Hank's struggling so much, no one else would want to buy the place unless they think they can get more out of the rent than Hank has been charging. And what if Donaldson agrees to pay the higher value of the land, giving Hank the deal he deserves, then jacks up the rent even more to make up for the added cost?"

Tessa sat down on the couch next to Samson, suddenly feeling deflated. She'd thought she had stumbled on a good solution to their problems, but Terry was making some really good points. They could save the gardens if her plan worked, but a lot of the tenants here could still lose their homes. A good number of the gardeners were older, retired people, like Terry and Mrs. Mackenzie, who lived on fixed incomes. They couldn't afford the kind of rent hike that a man like Donaldson would bring after he "upgraded" the apartment complex.

"What if..." Tessa said, tapping a finger against her lips as she thought it over. "What if we convinced them to offer discounted rent to the gardeners. We're providing a service to the complex. Our work improves the property value. Our work saves them money on landscaping costs. Plus things like the compost heap help to reduce waste, and that saves them money on waste removal. Shouldn't all of that effort be worth something?"

Samson put an arm around her shoulders, squeezing her tight. "In a perfect world? Yes, it would. But I really doubt you'll be able to sell that one. They'd see it as getting a discount for our 'hobby.'"

Tessa let out a frustrated sigh. She got up and walked over to the window, looking out at the gardens as the evening shadows extended over them. Orange and yellow dominated the landscape as pumpkins, squash, and other autumn crops grew across the gardens. Halloween decorations had been put up around some of the apartment doors, with straw scarecrows propped up on some back porches, and cardboard ghosts and skeletons hanging on windows and doors. There were almost no leaves on the ground, since the gardeners kept up with the raking throughout the season. They all put so much work and effort into maintaining their little community, but they didn't own it. That was the problem.

"I still want to talk to Hank," Tessa said. "Maybe he won't listen to everything, but even if he listens to just some of it, that could make a difference. It's not a perfect solution, but it's all we have. I would never forgive myself if I didn't try."

Samson stepped up behind her, putting his arms around her and leaning his chin on her shoulder. "All right," he said. "We'll head down there tomorrow and talk to him first thing. It's worth a shot."

She leaned back against him, smiling. "You really think we can make a difference?"

"I don't know," he said. "But we should try."

"That's why I love you." She reached up and caressed his cheek, then planted a soft kiss on his lips. For as long as she had known him, he had been a man who stood up for what was right.

She just hoped that their efforts wouldn't turn out to be in vain.

Chapter Seven

Tessa and Samson sat in Hank's office, waiting patiently while he looked over Tessa's report. He had been quiet for several minutes, though he had asked a few questions here and there for clarity. When he was done, he set down the report, cleared his throat, and looked up at the two of them.

"I can see you're really determined here," Hank said.

Tessa and Samson exchanged a look. "Yes," Tessa said. "We are. The gardening community means a lot to us. We might be a minority among the tenants, but we've formed a really strong bond over the years. And we all believe that what we have is something worth saving."

"And I respect that," Hank said. "I really do. But...I'm sorry."

"Come on, Hank," Samson said. "You won't even consider alternatives?"

"Look, I already knew Donaldson's offer wasn't what the property was really worth." Hank spread his hands, giving them an apologetic look. "But there's other factors you need to take into consideration. I'm desperate to get out from under this business. It's been turning south for years. Donaldson is offering me a way out, and enough money to pay off my debts and still have enough set aside afterwards that I won't have to work for a few years. Sure, maybe I could make the case to him that your gardens make the property more valuable. And I agree with you, they do. But this isn't about how much the property is worth. It's about how much I can get for it. And I'm desperate enough to take what I can get, that's just how it is."

Tessa's sat up straight. "We understand the position you're in. Isn't there anything we can do? Please, Hank."

Hank handed back her report. "Honestly, Tessa, you're not being fair to me here. I'm the one facing bankruptcy. I know your gardens are important to you, but I'm not going to ruin my finances in order to protect your hobby. That's my final word on this."

Tessa opened her mouth to protest further, but Samson put a hand on her knee, shaking his head. He gave her a sympathetic look, but she could see the defeat in his eyes.

Tessa sighed. She got up from her chair. "All right, Hank. Thank you for your time."

She and Samson left, then he walked her to her car so she could head to work. They stopped by the car and looked at each other. Tessa leaned her head against Samson's shoulder, fighting off tears. Part of her that thought she was being too emotional about this. It was just a garden, after all. But then, it was so much more than that. It was a place with history. A place of community. A place of friendship.

The place where they had fallen in love.

"We'll talk about some other options later," Samson said, stroking her hair. "We can still try meeting with Donaldson. I'm not ready to give up yet."

"Me neither," Tessa said. She smiled up at her man, feeling a sense of relief at his willingness to keep trying.

She pressed her lips against his, and they held each other for a long, intimate moment. Then she got into her car, while Samson got onto his bicycle to ride to his job at the music shop. Sometimes she felt guilty about polluting the atmosphere with her car's emissions when Samson went the extra mile by avoiding using a car whenever possible.

Though she did drive a hybrid, so that was a good compromise, at least. A balance between efficiency and environmentalism.

She drove out of the parking lot, looking over the apartments. About a dozen people were already in the gardens, people who were either retired or worked nights, and could therefore spend a weekday morning in the sunshine, working with the soil. A few kids, too young for school, were playing in front of one apartment while their mother watched them from the front step while reading a magazine. On the second and third floors, a few people were out on their balconies, enjoying the cool autumn weather. One woman had an easel out on her balcony, and she sat there painting a scene in autumn colors. Another woman was watering the flowers she had planted in a small planter that hung off the railing.

She wondered how many of those

people would also find their lives changed when Donaldson took over. Even the ones that weren't involved in the gardens would still be affected by the rent increase. How many of them would end up having to move out, so that new tenants with more money could move into Donaldson's "upgraded" apartments?

At work that day, whenever she had time in between her projects, Tessa did more research online. But all she ran into was dead ends. The law wasn't on her side, and it seemed like no one else was, either. No one except the small group of gardeners that were now her friends.

By the end of the day, she was so overwhelmed with all the information she'd been studying that she spent her last half hour just sitting at her desk, staring at the computer screen. She felt like a huge piece of her life was being taken away from her, and there was nothing she could do about it. And the worst part about it was how helpless she felt. Tessa had never been someone to stand aside and let something bad happen when there was something she could do about it. Sometimes she hadn't made the best decisions about how to handle things, but she always believed in acting. Yet she was at a loss as to what could be done.

When she got home, she went straight to Samson's apartment. As soon as he opened the door, she threw herself into his arms. He held her tight while she leaned against his shoulder and cried. He rubbed her back, whispering soothing words into her ear. Being there, with him, in his arms, helped her hold onto some hope that they would find a solution.

She looked up into his eyes, reaching up to caress his cheeks. He was so strong and supportive. She needed that. She needed, just for a little while, to feel like she wasn't losing control. To feel something other than the weight of the despair that had been settling over her for days on end.

She took his hand and led him to the sofa where they sat together, her head laying against Samson's chest so she could listen to his heartbeat.

She stayed awake long after Samson had drifted off to sleep, holding onto this moment for as long as she could. A while later she realized the deeper fear that had been lurking at the edges of her mind for days. The fear that she hadn't wanted to voice out loud.

If they lost not only the gardens, but their apartments, she and Samson would have to find new places to live. And she didn't know if they would end up in the same place together. They had never discussed moving in together. It hadn't seemed like an important thing to bring up, when they lived right down the hall from each other and each had keys to the other's apartment.

But if she had to find a new home, she wondered what would happen to her and Samson. Would he come with her? Would he move someplace else? And beyond all that, she wondered how it might change their relationship. They had known each other for years, living as close neighbors, before they became romantically involved. But sometimes, a foolish voice in the back of her head told her that it was a relationship of convenience. That Samson wouldn't stay interested in her if they were pulled further apart by the circumstances they now faced.

She knew it was a stupid thing to worry about. She was sure that Samson loved her, and that his feelings wouldn't change. But the sensible voice in her head that told her not to worry was slowly being drowned out by the paranoid voice that told her things were about to change. And those changes might spread to affect her entire life, from her garden to her home to the man that she loved.

Chapter Eight

At the end of the week, Hank sent out a letter to every apartment, announcing that he had officially sold the apartment complex to Donaldson Housing Enterprises. The letter was professional, even a bit apologetic, with Hank noting that the decision hadn't been an easy one. He also directed the tenants to bring any questions or concerns they had about their leases to Mr. Donaldson himself, since he would be the one making any and all decisions from that time on.

Tessa and the other members of the gardening community met once again to organize a protest against the gardens being torn down. They showed up at the office Saturday morning, more than two dozen of them this time, ready to bring their concerns to the new management. When they got to the office, Julie was there, working at her computer while a stack of papers slid out of the printer one by one. She looked up at them, a sympathetic frown on her face.

"Can I help you?" she asked. The look on her face told Tessa that she already knew what this was about.

"We'd like to speak with Mr. Donaldson, please," Tessa said.

Julie cleared her throat and folded her hands on her desk. "Mr. Donaldson said he's not taking complaints in person at this time, but he said you can send an email to the company account." Julie picked up one of the business cards from the little black holder on her desk, then held it out to Tessa.

Tessa took the card and frowned at it. She glanced behind her at the crowd of people, most of whom were still outside, since the office was too small for all of them. The cool autumn breeze coming from behind her through the propped-open door reminded her of the scale of their protest and the importance of what they were doing.

She stood up a bit straighter, refusing to back down. "I'm sorry, but we have to insist."

Julie spread her hands apologetically. "Tessa, there's nothing I can do. He already knows about your protest. Hank explained the whole thing to him before he left, so that Mr. Donaldson would be prepared to address it."

"And he's addressing it by ignoring us?" Tessa asked.

Julie sighed. She got up and stepped over to the printer, pulling out part of the stack of pages. The printer continuing whirring behind her, spewing out more pages in a steady stream. "I'm supposed to send a copy of this to every apartment. It's his official statement on the gardens."

Tessa took the pages, pulling off the top sheet to read and handing the others to Samson, who handed a few of them out to the other people in the crowd. Tessa scanned the page, her chest tightening with each line she read:

To: The residents of Maple Lane Apartments
RE: Upcoming changes
Dear Residents,
By now, most of you have no doubt heard that the apartment complex has recently been purchased by Donaldson Housing Enterprises. It is my goal, as the new administrator of these properties, to improve living conditions while simultaneously expanding the complex in order to attract new residents. At the same time, several policy changes are being implemented in order to reduce costs and increase the appeal to new residents. Beginning immediately, the following changes are

being put into effect for all residents:

- *Pet Policy: Dogs over fifty pounds are no longer permitted on the premises. Smaller dogs and cats must be registered with the office, including a monthly pet fee on your rent and a one-time nonrefundable pet cleaning deposit.*
- *Bicycles, toys, and other personal items may no longer be stored outdoors. Please store all personal property inside your apartment.*
- *Due to upcoming reconstruction of the parking lot, all residents will be given assigned parking spaces. Parking outside of your assigned spaces will result in a fine. A limited number of guest parking spaces will be reserved for any guests visiting your apartments.*

- *Gardening on the premises will no longer be permitted. Window and balcony planters are allowed provided they are well-secured. Existing gardens will be removed beginning Monday, October 31st in order to make room for new construction to begin this fall, expected to be completed spring of next year.*

No changes will be made to current leases at this time. Upon the expiration of your lease, a new lease will be offered, which will reflect additional changes to be implemented over the course of the next year.

Thank you for your time.
Chester Donaldson

"This is ridiculous!" Tessa said, waving the paper about angrily. "He's tearing down the gardens at the end of the month? He's treating us like this is a big joke."

"I don't know what to tell you, Tessa," Julie said, cringing in her seat. She twisted her pen nervously between her fingers. "I'm just the messenger. If you have a complaint, you'll have to email Mr. Donaldson with it. There's nothing I can do."

Tessa clenched her fists, crumpling Donaldson's letter in her hand. She knew that none of this was Julie's fault so she tried not to cause a scene.

Tessa gestured towards the back office, which used to be Hank's. "Is he here, now?"

"I'm sorry, he's not," Julie said. "He's overseeing the purchase of several other properties. We're getting a new apartment manager at the beginning of next month, to oversee day to day operations. But whoever that is, they'll be reporting to Mr. Donaldson."

Tessa huffed, but she knew there was

nothing else to be done. For now, at least. "All right, Julie. Thank you."

She turned and left, and the group gathered outside in a loose circle, talking among themselves. Several people started asking what they should do next, and a bunch of suggestions were tossed around.

"Everyone," Tessa said, holding up her hands to get their attention. "For now, I think the best thing we can do is make our voices be heard. Everyone should write an email, or even better, a physical letter, voicing our protests. If Donaldson hears from enough tenants, he might be willing to change his mind."

There was some more discussion about that idea, with several people protesting that it wouldn't end up doing any good. But most people seemed to think it was worth an effort. The group eventually broke apart, with everyone returning to their own apartments. Tessa and Samson headed back to her place, and they spent the next hour drafting a letter to Mr. Donaldson, trying to make it as professional and persuasive as possible.

After the letter was finished, Tessa leaned back in her chair, feeling spent and exhausted. Samson stepped up behind her, rubbing her shoulders. "It's going to be okay," he said.

"You don't know that."

"I do," Samson said. "I don't know what will happen with the gardens, but I do know that in the long run, things will be okay. We just need to have faith."

Tessa reached up and squeezed Samson's hand. She wished that she had his faith. But she was starting to believe that they were out of options.

She would need to think of something more drastic to do, or else the gardens would be gone by the end of the month. And when Donaldson carried out his plan, many of her friends would be gone too.

Chapter Nine

As the month began to draw to a close, there was still no progress made in protecting the gardens. Donaldson replied to all of the emails with a form letter, pointing out that the gardeners didn't own the land they had been working for years, and stating that he would understand if any tenants decided to leave the complex to find someplace else to live.

A few of the gardeners started harvesting the rest of their crops early, seeming to have given up. But most of them stood strong, continuing to go out every day to tend to their plots, clinging to the hope that they wouldn't be forced to give up something they loved doing.

Tessa's pumpkins came in quite

nicely, and she let several of the neighborhood children come by to pick out pumpkins to carve for Halloween. A few days later, when she saw the Jack O' Lanterns burned bright on her neighbors' front steps, she took it as a silent protest to Donaldson's new rules and restrictions. It made her want to keep looking for some way to save their community.

A few days before the demolition of the gardens was scheduled, Tessa was out in her garden with Samson and a few of the others. She sat on an old tree stump that stood near one end of the garden, sipping some of Samson's herbal tea. A gloom hung over the group.

"I may be moving out at the end of next month," Terry said. He stood with his shoulders slumped, looking out over the gardens with a wistful look in his eyes.

"Already?" Tessa asked. "I'd hate to see you go." She'd grown close to the old man over the last few months. He was beginning to feel like family.

"My lease expires the end of November," Terry said. "Donaldson offered me a new one, but the rent is hiked up so much, I don't see how I could afford it. Not a lot of options for someone like me. I've been talking to a cousin of mine, might be able to work something out to stay in his spare room."

"Where does he live?" Tessa asked.

"Upstate, near New York."

"That's so far away." Tessa stared into her tea, feeling lost. It didn't seem right. But when it came down to it, they were all people without power. Donaldson owned the property, and he could set whatever terms he wanted to in the new leases he was offering. It wouldn't matter to him if half of his tenants were driven out by the rent hike. He'd find more people willing to pay the higher rates, and he'd rake in the profits.

"We'll keep in touch," Samson said. "I'll make sure of that."

"Yes, I'm sure we will," Terry said, though his voice lacked conviction. He stared off into the distance, and for a moment Tessa thought she saw tears welling in his dark eyes. He shook his head and turned away. "I'm going to head in early today. I'm...I'm tired."

"Take care, Terry," Samson said.

Tessa just watched him go. She felt the same weight on her that she could see bearing down on Terry's shoulders.

"I think I'm going to head in, too," Samson said, patting Tessa's shoulder. "We should go out tomorrow night. Have a night off. Enjoy ourselves."

"Yeah, that sounds good," Tessa said, without any excitement in her voice.

Samson leaned down and kissed the top of her head, then he picked up the half-empty pitcher of tea and headed back to his apartment.

Tessa sat there alone for a few

minutes, looking out over the gardens. People were still tending their plots, despite knowing they'd be gone in a few days. She drank the last of her tea, then set the glass down in the dirt. It was getting chilly outside, and she knew she needed to go in soon, but she didn't have the energy to get up. She wanted to stay where she was, enjoying what time she had left of her home.

"You think they're gonna tear down those trees, too?" a voice asked.

Tessa turned and saw Topher standing a few feet away. He nodded towards the tree line at the far end of the apartment, where a few men from the demolition company were surveying the land. They had been around the complex for a few days now, using their surveying equipment to measure the available space, all in preparation for the day the bulldozers arrived. While Tessa and Topher watched, one of the men took out a can of red spray paint and started spraying large X's on several of the trees, presumably marking which ones would be cut down.

"The new building is supposed to extend all the way down into the woods," Tessa said. "Right up to the fence." There was a small convenience store on the other side of the woods, and a chain link fence marked the border between the apartment complex's property and the store's. There was a large hole torn through the fence. Tessa had used it as a short cut on more than one occasion, since it was faster to cut through the woods than it was to walk out to the street and circle around.

She remembered one day, when she had been heading to the store to get a sandwich and some juice, she had found the fence repaired. Hank had sent the maintenance crew out to patch up the hole in it, blocking off the short cut. She had been irritated at the inconvenience. It had been so pointless to keep the area fenced off, when the rest of the apartment complex was open, and so many of the tenants cut through the back way to get where they were going.

A few days later, she had seen one of her neighbors heading through the woods to the short cut again. She had expected them to be turned back, but when they didn't return, she walked back into the woods and saw that someone—presumably one of her neighbors—had cut a new hole in the fence. And while it was an act of vandalism and Tessa knew she shouldn't have been happy about it, she hadn't been able to help feeling glad that it had happened.

Hank had tried to repair the fence again once after that, only to have it cut open again. After that, he'd given up. It seemed like such a small thing, but in a way it reminded Tessa that people couldn't always force you to do what they said.

"It's such a shame," Topher said, shaking his head at the men by the trees. "Those trees have been there for decades, and now they're being cut down to build more apartments. Pretty soon this whole area won't have any nature left."

Tessa shrugged. "But then again, this whole area used to be wooded. Most of the state still is. If no one ever cut down any trees, none of us would have homes to live in."

Topher scowled, pulling down the wall of tarps he'd put up around his garden patch. "Maybe," he said. "But that doesn't mean they need to tear down *those* trees. Those are *our* trees."

Tessa looked down at the stump she was sitting on. It had been here for as long as she'd lived in the apartment complex, and she didn't know what had happened to the tree that had once stood here. Had it been cut down? Knocked over in a storm? Or had it simply died?

She might never know. But it was still here. A few of the gardeners had tried to dig it up once, a year or two ago, but it was too thick and the roots rug too deep. Though she was sure that when the bulldozers came, they'd have no trouble getting it out.

She ran her hand along the smooth, worn surface of the stump. It was as stubborn as they came, but it would still end up having to face the music when the time came.

As she tapped her fingers on the old wood, a thought occurring to her. She bit her lower lip, wondering if she could actually do it. It was crazy, but then, most of her schemes tended to be crazy. At least this time, however, she knew that it was for a good cause.

"You know what, Topher?" she asked, getting up and brushing off her pants. "You're right. They don't need to tear it down. Any of it."

She headed back to her apartment to

fetch her car keys. She drove down to Home Depot, then wandered around the store for a few minutes, a bit lost. She was never much of a home improvement person. Eventually, one of the store clerks noticed the lost look on her face and came over to help.

"Can I help you find something, miss?"

"Yes," she said, a proud smile on her face. "I need to buy a padlock, and some of the thickest chain you've got."

Chapter Ten

When Tessa got home, she dug through her closet until she found the little handheld Igloo cooler she used when she went to picnics and other outdoor events. She went through her cabinets and pulled out whatever nonperishable goods she could find: granola bars, cans of mixed nuts, packs of peanut butter crackers, and a variety of other snacks. She loaded all of it into the cooler then took it, along with a mostly-full twenty-four pack of bottled water, and headed out to the stump at the edge of the gardens.

She set an old pillow down on the ground by the stump, along with her food and water. She pulled out the heavy chain she'd bought and looped it around the tree stump, making sure to secure it nice and tight so that it wouldn't budge. Then she settled down onto her pillow and looped the chain around her body, criss-crossing it over her shoulders and across her chest. She locked the chain in place and tucked the key into her bra. Then she settled in to wait.

The first few hours sitting there in the dark were cold and boring. She scrolled through the Twitter app on her phone for a little while, then snapped a couple of selfies of herself chained to the stump. She didn't expect to get much response, other than a few out of state friends who ended up asking her what she was doing, then telling her she was crazy.

She slept for a little while, though it was hard to sleep well when she was chained to a tree stump on a frigid October night. She woke up with a sore back early in the morning, when some of her neighbors were starting to wake up.

The first person to notice her was one

of her neighbor's children. She pointed right at Tessa and asked, "Mommy, what's she doing?"

The neighbor looked at Tessa. Tessa waved at her. The woman gave her an awkward wave back, then she hurried her daughter along, leaning over to whisper to her as they walked.

Topher was one of the first gardeners up for the day. He was out not long after the sun rose, heading straight for his little patch of the garden. He barely glanced at Tessa at first, then he did a double take when he noticed the chains. "Tessa?" he asked. "Dude, are you okay?"

"I'm fine," Tessa said, smiling up at him from her seat. "A bit cold and sore, but it's worth it."

He took in the sight of her chained to the stump, a dumbfounded look on his face. "You...did you do this to yourself?"

"Yeah. I'm protesting." She folded her hands in her lap, a proud grin on her face.

"That's..." He ran his hand through his hair, letting out a long, slow breath. "Wow. I don't know if that's brilliant or crazy. How long have you been there?"

"Since last night."

"And how long are you staying?"

"Until Donaldson agrees to let us keep the gardens."

"Wow." Topher looked at the chains again, as if he was having trouble accepting what he was seeing. "Well, damn. Good for you, then. Do you...do you need anything?"

"Well..." Tessa shifted a bit uncomfortably where she sat. "I did forget one thing."

"What's that?"

She looked over her shoulder to make sure no one else was in earshot, then lowered her voice. "I kind of forgot to figure out a way to go to the bathroom."

"Oh. Oh. Damn. Umm." Topher looked around, running a hand through his hair. "Wait, okay, I gotcha. Hold on a minute."

He went to his back door and gathered up the tarps he'd used as a wall around his garden, before he'd taken them down. He hammered a few waist-high wooden stakes into the ground in a square around Tessa, then tied the tarps to them, forming a low series of walls. Then he brought her a couple of empty bottles. "Best I can do, I guess."

"Thanks, Topher." She took the bottles, along with an extra tarp Topher brought her that she could drape over herself for extra privacy. It was a bit awkward and difficult, but she managed to make it work with just a little bit of mess. She just hoped she wouldn't have to be out here long before she got Donaldson to agree to her demands. Luckily Topher was nice enough to bring her some tissue and hand sanitizer, along with a plastic garbage bag.

Later in the morning, more and more

of her neighbors started gathering around. They all questioned her about what she was doing, and some of them called her crazy, while others offered their support. A few even sat down with her to show their solidarity with her cause. Around mid-morning, Terry came out with one of his couch cushions and a thermos full of coffee. He settled down next to her, poured her some coffee in a paper cup, and they chatted casually while they waited for the inevitable.

"So," Terry said, sipping at his coffee. "Donaldson know you're here yet?"

"I'm sure he'll hear about it soon," Tessa said. She held the paper cup cradled in her hands, warming them up. "I'm kind of scared, but a bit excited."

"You know he's gonna have you arrested, right?" Terry glanced at her with an expression of pride on his face.

"Maybe," Tessa said. "But I think it's worth it. Imagine the publicity. I'm sure it'll end up on the news. If it's enough to convince Donaldson to let us keep the gardens, or to sell the complex to someone who doesn't want to tear the place down to build another building, then it'll be worth it."

"I hope so." Terry patted her on the knee. "But I'd find a good lawyer, just in case. I believe in what you're doing, trying to save our community. I just don't want to see you end up in jail over it."

Tessa took Terry's hand and squeezed it. She knew he had been in prison, so he certainly had a unique perspective on it.

It was afternoon before Samson arrived, returning home from a morning shift at the music shop. He rode his bicycle around the back of the buildings, then stopped and got off, looking at Tessa and shaking his head. He strolled over to her with a bemused expression on his face, then sat down cross-legged on the ground in front of her. "Well," he said, "I got a call at work today that you were up to something, but I had to see it for myself."

Tessa grinned, sitting up a bit straighter. The chains chafed a bit, though the thick material of her jacket kept them from being too uncomfortable. "I told you I was going to do something."

"I wasn't expecting something this crazy." He looked her up and down, taking in the chains and the short wall of tarps that surrounded her. She'd opened up the front of the privacy wall for now, though she wasn't looking forward to the awkward moment in a couple of hours when she had to make use of it again.

"What can I say." Tessa shrugged. "I guess I must be nuts."

"At least you're nuts for a good reason."

"Well, here's hoping that—"

Tessa cut off in mid-sentence when she saw the flashing lights of a police car pulling into the parking lot. A few moments later, two police officers started walking towards her, with Mr. Donaldson at their side. Donaldson stopped a few feet from Tessa, planting his fists on his hips and frowning at her. He took in the rest of the crowd; a dozen people had joined Tessa on the ground. "I don't know what you're hoping to accomplish here," Donaldson said, "but this ends now. Get up, all of you, and return to your homes, and I won't press charges."

"Press charges for breaking what law?" Tessa asked, raising her chin. "Sitting in our own backyards?"

"Don't give me that," Donaldson said. "I own this property, and I've given you all written notice about the removal of the gardens. You can't be here."

"What about our first amendment rights?" Terry asked. "We're here for a formal protest. Besides, your 'written notice' only said the gardens are being removed. It didn't say we lost the right to sit and enjoy the sunshine in our own backyards."

"This is ridiculous," Donaldson said. He looked at the two cops, gesturing angrily to the protesters. "Gentlemen, have all of these people arrested."

One of the cops stepped forward, clearing his throat. He adjusted his hat and said, "I'm not sure we can do that."

"What do you mean?" Donaldson shouted. He pointed accusingly at Tessa. "She's trespassing. They're all trespassing!"

"Well, sir," the cop said, "they do live here. I'm not sure we can remove people forcefully from their own homes. It would be one thing if they were blocking the streets, that's a clear violation of the law. But I'm not sure we could charge people with trespassing in their own backyards."

"Preposterous!" Donaldson threw his hands up in the air. His face started to turn red as he yelled. "I own this property, and I say they're trespassing."

"I understand that, sir. But you also have lease agreements with everyone here, correct? I believe that gives them the right to be here."

"So you're not going to do anything?" Donaldson leaned forward, sticking his face right in the cop's.

"It's a complicated situation," the cop said. "I'm gonna have to call this in for advisement on how to proceed."

The cop walked a short distance off and spoke into the radio strapped to his shoulder. Donaldson glared at Tessa and the others, clenching and unclenching his fists. Then he stalked off.

Tessa and the other protesters applauded. They had won the first round.

Chapter Eleven

Tessa remained chained to the stump all day and all night. Her neighbors took turns sitting out with her, some of them returning to the warmth of their apartments for a few hours, only to return later with food, hot coffee, and anything else they could bring to make the hours pass more easily. Samson even took her cell phone back inside to charge at one point, so that she could keep news of the protest going on social media in order to gain more support.

Monday morning, the day the demolition was scheduled, Tessa woke to the sounds of loud engines rumbling. She had slept uncomfortably, with pillows and a sleeping bag Samson had brought her. With several pillows leaned up against the tree stump, it hadn't been so bad, even though her back was sore and she desperately needed to get up and walk around to stretch her unused muscles.

When she opened her eyes, she saw a large yellow bulldozer parked a dozen feet in front of her. Several police cars were parked in the parking lot, and a handful of cops lingered nearby, monitoring the situation without interfering. A news van had also arrived, and the camera crew was setting up to record the ongoing protest.

Tessa shifted in her seat while the reporter and cameraman approached her. Her hair was a mess, she hadn't bathed, and she needed to pee pretty badly, but now clearly wasn't the time. She straightened her hair as best she could and sat up straight, giving the reporter a welcoming smile as she approached.

The reporter sat right down on the

ground next to Tessa, extending her hand. "Hello. Tracy Williams, Channel Five News. I'd like to interview you for the morning broadcast."

Tessa shook the woman's hand. "Nice to meet you. I'm Tessa, and I'm here to protest the destruction of our community garden." Tessa raised her chin, proud that what she was doing had finally drawn the right kind of attention.

"We'll be going on the air soon," Tracy said. "In the meantime, I'd like to ask you a few questions off camera so we can get the facts straight. Then we'll go over it all again formally once we go live. Is that all right?"

Tessa beamed. "Absolutely."

The reporter spent a few minutes taking notes as she asked Tessa for some details about the protest and how it had started. Then she spoke by radio to the anchors back at the news station, getting everything ready for the live broadcast. She signaled for Tessa to wait, while she listened through her earpiece to what the anchors were saying back in the studio. When they were ready to go, she gave Tessa a nod, then looked up at the camera and started to speak into her microphone.

"I'm here with Tessa Cunningham, resident of Maple Lane Apartments and avid gardener. As you can see, she's here today, after chaining herself to a tree stump to sit in protest of the impending destruction of her community garden. Tessa, can you tell us what prompted this protest, and what you're hoping to accomplish here today?"

Tessa looked into the camera, then noticed Mr. Donaldson standing nearby, glaring at her. He crossed his arms and stared her down, his frown deepening with each passing moment. Tessa smiled. If Donaldson was this unhappy with what was going on, she counted it as a win.

"Yes, Tracy," Tessa said. "I've lived

here for years and have been part of a wonderful gardening community that has developed among the neighbors here at the apartment complex. We've all poured our hearts and our souls into developing these gardens, and it's been a wonderful experience that has brought all of us closer together. But just this past month, we found out that the apartment complex was being bought out by a man named Donaldson, and as new owner, he decided without any input from us or any consideration for the residents of this community that he was going to tear down our gardens to put up a new apartment building. He refused to listen to reason or work with us for any kind of compromise, so I decided that I needed to take action in order to protect something I've helped nurture and grow for years."

"So your goal is to halt the new construction that's scheduled to begin today?" Tracy asked.

"It doesn't have to halt," Tessa said. "We just don't want the construction to come at the cost of our gardens. There's plenty of other places where Mr. Donaldson could put up a new building, places where he wouldn't need to destroy something we've all worked so hard for over the years. And while, yes, he may own the land now, he's not the one who has put his time and his heart and soul into this land for such a long time. We don't think it's fair for our gardens, which we were given permission to plant by the previous owner, to be taken from us without us having any say in it."

"Thank you so much, Tessa," Tracy said. She turned back to the camera. "There you have it. A community coming together to protect something they've worked so hard for. Mr. Donaldson has so far declined to give us a statement on this matter, but Channel Five News will keep you updated on how the events here at Maple Lane play out."

After the camera cut, Tessa shook the woman's hand again. "Thank you. Thank you so much for helping us get the word out about this."

"Good luck," Tracy said. "I can't imagine doing something like this. You've got moxie, girl."

The reporter and the camera man went off to interview some of the other neighbors to get footage for the later followup report. Donaldson was still glaring at Tessa. She just smiled at him, folding her hands in her lap. Finally, he came over to talk to her again. He stood above her, glowering down at her.

"I can still have you arrested, you know," he said. "I might not be able to technically have you removed for trespassing, but now you're obstructing the construction project and interfering with my rights as the property owner."

"How is it going to look on the news if you have me hauled off in handcuffs?"

Tessa asked, smiling smugly at him. "You think it might make it hard for you to find new tenants to move into the new building you're putting up?"

Donaldson ground his teeth. He glanced at the reporter, then at the crowd that had gathered to watch what was happening. The crowd was slowly growing. It looked like people from outside the apartment complex were starting to get interested in what was going on.

Donaldson crouched down so he could look Tessa in the eye. "All right. What's it going to take to put an end to this?"

"Let us keep the gardens," Tessa said.

"I can't do that. I've already invested too much in this project. I've put a deposit with the construction crew, and I've already got contracts with several other developers for the refurbishing of the existing buildings. There's no way I can just pull the plug on this."

J.L. STARR   331

Tessa bit her lower lip. As much as she thought of this man as her enemy, she didn't want to destroy his business. She just wanted her community to remain intact. There had to be a way to get both. "Can't you build somewhere else?"

"There's no other suitable site," Donaldson said. He gestured back to the tree line. "There's not enough room back at the edge of the property for an entire building without encroaching on the neighboring property. And we can't build on the south end of the property because of the stream that passes through the woods there. It's part of the local waterways and we're not allowed to touch it."

Tessa frowned, looking around. The complex was fairly small, and it was true that there wasn't much more space.

"What if," Donaldson asked, "I let you do your gardening someplace else. It doesn't have to be right here, does it?"

Tessa touched a finger to her lips,

thinking it over. "There's not going to be enough room with the new building here. And it's not like we can garden back in the woods. There's no sunlight."

Donaldson let out a long sigh. He gestured to the backs of the buildings. "What if I let you set up raised garden beds along the sides of the buildings, and around the back. You can't dig into the ground that close to the foundation, but raised beds would be acceptable. You can circle the buildings with them if you want. I'll clear out the space. We'd have to set some kind of limitations. Nothing too close to the air conditioning units, that sort of thing. But honestly, that's the best I can do."

Tessa glanced back that way, thinking it over. It wouldn't quite be the same. But raised beds, lined up alongside the building, would actually give them more space than they had right now. It would be a substantial change, but it would let them keep their community intact.

J.L. STARR   333

"What about the rent?" Tessa asked. "Not everyone needs these upgrades you're planning on. No one wants to be forced out of their homes just so you can put in stainless steel kitchens and charge extra rent for making things look modern."

Donaldson huffed. He braced his hands on his knees, and for a moment she thought he was going to get up and walk away. "I can't freeze the rent," he said. "But there is something to be said for the loyalty of long term residents. I can see about *limiting* the increase for...let's say anyone who's been here five years or more. Beyond that, it just doesn't make good business sense when I can get new tenants in here who are happy to pay more for a more modern apartment."

Tessa thought it over. It felt like a victory. Not a complete one, but compromise was better than nothing.

"I need an answer on this, Miss

Cunningham," Donaldson said. "I want to end this. I'm willing to meet you part way."

"I need to discuss it with my fellow gardeners," Tessa said.

Donaldson rolled his eyes. He pushed to his feet. "Fine. Make it quick."

He walked away, and Tessa waved excitedly to Samson and the others who stood nearby. They gathered around, and she explained Donaldson's terms to them.

"Raised beds?" Samson asked, rubbing his chin. "I don't see any problem with that. It'd be a bit of effort to set up. But I think it's a good plan."

"It would certainly save my back," Terry said, snorting. "Not having to bend over to reach the dirt."

They discussed it for a few more minutes, but everyone seemed to agree that it was a fair compromise. Tessa waved Donaldson over. She folded her hands in her lap and said, "We all agree.

J.L. STARR   335

We'd just like it in writing."

"Fine. Whatever it takes to end this."

Tessa pulled out the key and unlocked herself from the chains. She stood up, stretching her aching muscles. The crowd gathered around started to applaud.

Donaldson stalked off after agreeing to a time for them to come to his office and get the agreement in writing. The reporter came over to ask Tessa what happened. But Tessa could barely think clearly enough to give the interview. Her head was spinning and her heart swelled with pride about what she had just done.

Though after more than a day sitting outside chained to a tree stump, more than anything she really needed to go inside and take a long, hot shower.

Chapter Twelve

By the time winter passed and spring came back around, the construction of the new apartment building was well under way. Tessa and her neighbors worked busily setting up their new raised gardens in preparation for the first planting of the season. Samson and a few others who had good, strong backs were hauling wheelbarrows full of luscious black organically-fertilized soil, which the community had all pitched in for. They shoveled the new soil into the new waist-high raised garden beds that lined the entire width of the apartment building, and the smell of fresh earth filled the air.

Tessa's raised beds, each the size of a large dining room table, stood on either side of her apartment's back door. One was nestled right outside her kitchen window, and she had decided that this year, she would dedicate that one to growing flowering herbs like silver thyme, ornamental oregano, and rosemary. She had already divided her garden bed into different sections to allow for the differences in soil that each plant thrived best in, and she was looking forward to seeing the plants bloom outside her window while their scent filled the air.

She was also planning to add some carrots, beets, and radishes to her other bed, since root vegetables like those thrived so well in an environment that was free of rocks and other debris that might hinder their growth.

Samson rolled a wheelbarrow over to her new beds, setting it down, then leaning against the wall to catch his breath. He had his shirt off while he worked in the sun, and Tessa was quite appreciative of the sight of her man covered in a light, glistening sheen of sweat while he worked to help rebuild the gardens in their new form. She stepped over to him and leaned her arms around his shoulders, pursing her lips and looking into his eyes.

"You don't need to set up my beds first," she said. "What about the ones by your apartment?"

"Well," Samson said, "about that..."

"What?" Tessa leaned back, a concerned look on her face.

"Well," he said, "I just got my lease renewal from Donaldson. And since I've only lived here a little over four and a half years, I didn't qualify for the discounted rent he promised to long-term tenants."

"Oh no." Tessa felt her heart starting to race. "You're...you're not moving, are you?"

"Well, I wanted to talk to you about that."

"About you moving?" Tessa frowned.

"Well, I was thinking," he said. "Since both of our rents are going to be going up, but we spend so much time at each other's apartments anyway..."

Tessa blinked, then a smile slowly spread across her lips. "Samson, are you asking to move in with me?"

He grinned, slipping his arms around her waist. "What do you think?"

She leaned in and kissed him, slow and sweet. She pulled back and looked into his eyes. "I think it's a wonderful idea."

Samson's grin widened.

"There's just one thing," Tessa said.

"What's that?"

Tessa smirked and poked him in the chest. "You'd better get your own garden beds, mister. Just because I'm sharing my home with you doesn't mean you can plant your herbs in my dirt."

He laughed and put his arms around her. They held each other close, savoring the moment, while the neighbor kids ran by, laughing and playing, and the gardeners worked hard at their preparations, rebuilding the gardens and sharing in the community that they all loved.

THE END

TESSA'S WINTER

Tessa's Winter

Chapter One

Tessa was all set to move in with her boyfriend and start the next important stage of their relationship together, when she got a very unexpected phone call from her mother.

She answered the phone while she was in the middle of making dinner: brown rice and stir-fried vegetables grown in the garden beds outside her apartment. She was expecting her boyfriend, Samson, to be home any minute, but it wasn't like she could just cut short a phone call with her mother.

They barely saw each other anymore. Not since her parents had moved to Florida.

"Hi, Mom," she said, cradling the phone against her shoulder while she stirred the vegetables. "What's up?"

"Oh, Tessa. Oh..."

Tessa frowned, pausing in her cooking. It sounded like her mother was crying. "Mom? Is everything okay?"

"No, everything's not okay. Your father..."

Tessa's heart leapt up into her throat, the worst possibilities immediately springing to mind.

"...is such an *ass!*"

Tessa closed her eyes, rubbing her forehead. She took a few deep breaths to calm herself down. "Mom, hold on. What happened? Are you and Dad okay?"

"No, we're really not," her mother said. "He's been so distant lately. He's been working such long hours. He never

TESSA'S WINTER

pays any attention to me anymore. And frankly, sometimes I worry that he might be...might be...seeing someone else."

Tessa rolled her eyes. This wasn't the first time her mother had been paranoid about Dad, but Tessa was one hundred percent sure that her father wasn't cheating. For one thing, he simply wasn't the type. For another thing, her mother's alleged reasons for her suspicions were always vague and unfounded, like being worried about Dad working long hours, then later finding out he had actually been working late in order to save up money for a big vacation. Tessa had no doubt that her mother's concerns would be equally unfounded this time.

"Mom, I'm sure everything will be fine," Tessa said, turning her attention back to cooking dinner. "Dad loves you, you know that."

"I don't think it's going to be that

simple this time. I think...I think maybe we need some time apart."

"That's just crazy, Mom," Tessa said. "You just need to take a few days to think things over. Spend some time working on your cross stitch projects, that always gives you plenty of time to think."

The apartment door opened and Samson stepped inside, carrying a bag of groceries in one hand and a sheaf of paper in the other. He smiled at Tessa, holding the papers up to show them to her. Tessa smiled back, pointing at her phone and mouthing the words, *my mother*.

Samson nodded, keeping quiet so as not to interrupt the conversation, and he started putting the groceries away.

"I don't think it's going to be that simple this time, Tessa," her mother repeated. "I really do think we need some time apart."

Tessa sighed. She looked at Samson

and rolled her eyes. Samson shrugged sympathetically. She knew *he* never had to deal with this sort of stuff from his mother.

"So take a little vacation," Tessa suggested. "Just for you. You can afford to take some time off of work, right?"

Her mother had worked for years at a little Hallmark shop, making a modest income. Her father had insisted for years that she didn't "need" to work, clinging to the old-fashioned idea that the man was supposed to be the bread winner. And when Tessa had been younger, her mom had stayed home from work to take care of her. But once Tessa had moved out on her own, her mother had been determined to get back to working again, insisting that she would go crazy if she sat home alone all day.

"I was actually thinking about coming up there to see you," Mom said.

Tessa looked at Samson, her eyes wide

with panic. She set down the spoon, suddenly forgetting about dinner. "Uhh, Mom, I don't know if that's the best idea right now. Samson and I, well, things are getting pretty serious."

"Oh, Samson seems like such a nice young man. You know, I really would like to come up there and finally meet him."

"Yeah, he's amazing. I really love him, Mom."

Clearly unaware of exactly what was being said on the other end of the phone, Samson stood up a bit straighter, a comically smug look on his face. He straightened his shirt and raised his chin, then started smoothing out his hair, acting like some kind of teenager before a hot date. Tessa had to cover her mouth with her hand to keep from laughing out loud at his antics.

"Well, then I can meet him when I come up there," her mother said. "I was thinking about driving up next week."

"Next week?" Tessa gave Samson a worried look.

Apparently misinterpreting what Tessa was saying, Samson nodded eagerly and grabbed the sheaf of papers he'd brought home with him. He held them up to show Tessa. It was his expired leasing agreement. They had been talking about moving in together, and Samson had let his lease expire so he could move in to Tessa's apartment. He was supposed to move in next week, though he practically lived there already, with how much time he spent at Tessa's place.

"Yes, I thought I'd take the bus up. You know I don't like driving that far these days. You still have that pull-out couch, right?"

Tessa chewed on her lip, silently pleading to Samson with her eyes. Not picking up on her concern, Samson smiled, and he started tearing the old lease in half. Then he threw the pieces

J.L. STARR

up in the air triumphantly, practically dancing with excitement.

Tessa gave him a more urgent look, and in a tone meant more for Samson than for her mother, she said, "You want to come up here to stay with me? Next week?"

Samson's smile disappeared. He looked down at the torn up bits of his old lease, frowning in concern.

"Don't worry dear," her mother said, "I won't be in the way. I can spend some time out in that garden you're always raving about. And I can catch up on my cross stitch, like you said."

Tessa rubbed a hand over her face. She looked up at Samson, desperate. He gave her a helpless shrug, holding his hands out to either side.

Tessa let out a frustrated sigh. "Yeah, okay Mom. That...that sounds great."

Samson's shoulders slumped. He started gathering up the torn fragments of his old lease.

"I'll let you know when I'll be there, after I check the bus schedules. I'll probably come into Philly. Oh, maybe when I get there, we can go see the city! It's been years since I've been to Philadelphia. And let me tell you, dear, you simply cannot get a good cheesesteak down here in Florida."

"Great, Mom," Tessa said, slumping down into a chair. "I'll see you then."

"Excellent. Take care of yourself, Tessa. I'll see you soon. Love you."

"Love you too."

Tessa hung up the phone. She looked up at Samson, feeling deflated.

"So," Samson said, holding the torn up lease in his hands, "your mother is coming."

As if in response, the smoke detector went off, filling the apartment with a loud, shrill beep. Tessa had forgotten about the food on the stove, and a thick stream of greasy smoke was rising from the pan.

Tessa grabbed the pan and moved it off the heat, opening a window and waving a towel in the air to clear the smoke. Samson waved the lease papers over the smoke detector like a fan, trying to silence it. Finally he pulled it down from the ceiling and pulled the battery out.

Tessa slumped against the counter. "Yes," she said. "Yes, my mother is coming."

Chapter Two

What was originally supposed to be a two-week visit turned into two months, then into six months, and Tessa slowly started to lose her mind. At first, she thought her mother was just going through a period of depression, and she spent the first couple of weeks trying to convince her mother to forgive Dad and go back to him. But when her mother decided, a few weeks after coming up to New Jersey, to apply for a transfer to a local Hallmark store, Tessa started to realize just how serious the situation was. Her mother started working part time at the local store, and when her paychecks started coming in, she opened a new, independent bank account, to keep her money separate from the joint checking account she shared with Dad. Then, as more time passed, she started nesting and making friends with Tessa's neighbors. She even joined the Scrabble club that her neighbors, Mrs. Mackenzie and Terry Jones, attended at the local church every Wednesday night.

Tessa had been dragged down to the Scrabble club one night, just after Thanksgiving. She was losing the game pretty badly. She had a decent enough vocabulary, but the club members apparently shared all kinds of advanced techniques, like knowing how to block off your opponent's access to the Triple Word Score spaces, and how to use a lot of obscure little two-letter words to rack up points horizontally and vertically at the same time. As a result, everyone else at the table was over a hundred points, when Tessa barely had fifty.

Her mother put down a word, and Tessa frowned at it, tilting her head to read the board better. "Xi?" Tessa asked, not even sure if she was pronouncing it correctly. "That's so not a word."

"Fourteenth letter of the Greek alphabet," her mother said, sitting up a bit straighter, a proud smile on her face. "And with X on the Triple Letter Score, that's twenty-five points."

Tessa frowned, thinking of challenging it, but she didn't want to waste her turn if she turned out to be wrong. She let out a long sigh, looking at her own tiles. Finally she put an O on the board. "Ox. Nine points."

Her mother's smile widened. One thing about her mother was that she'd always been very competitive, never letting Tessa win at games unless she earned it, even when she was a kid. It could be a bit frustrating at times.

Her phone beeped with an incoming text. She grabbed it and swiped her finger across the screen, reading the text.

J.L. STARR

"No cheating now," Terry said with a friendly smile. "You can't be looking words up on your phone."

"It's Samson," Tessa said. She wouldn't have used her phone to cheat at Scrabble, though it *was* a bit tempting, now that she was more than seventy-five points behind her mother's score.

She read the text while Terry took his turn: *Hey. Dinner tonight?*

Tessa chewed on her lower lip, glancing sidelong at her mother. Her relationship with Samson had been put through some strain since her mother moved in. For one thing, it had indefinitely postponed their plans to move in together. Samson had been forced to stay in a friend's basement, since he'd already given up his apartment before Tessa's mother moved in with her. They had expected at first that Samson would only be staying at his friend's house for a couple of weeks, but that had been before her mother's visit had turned into a six month long stay. They had discussed more than once what to do, whether Samson should get himself a new apartment, or whether Tessa needed to convince her mother to move out on her own. But Samson didn't want to get a new apartment and be stuck in a lease, not when he had his heart set on moving in with Tessa. And Tessa could never quite broach the subject of making her mother move out.

She glanced at the board when Terry turned her "Ox" into "Jukebox" with the K on a Triple Letter Score for a total of thirty-seven points. Tessa shook her head in disbelief and texted Samson back: *I'm stuck at Scrabble night with Mom. I don't think we're getting done until 8:00.*

"How's Samson doing, dear?" her mother asked. "We hardly see him anymore."

"He's doing good," Tessa said. She

wanted to add, *he barely comes over anymore because you're in bed by 9:30 and you complain if we're making too much noise,* but she bit her tongue.

Scrabble night wasn't the time to start complaining about her living arrangement with her mother. Though she was starting to wonder when the right time would be. Any time Tessa tried to bring it up, her mother made excuses. She said she loved how much time they got to spend together now, or that she wasn't sure about getting her own place since she hadn't decided whether she was staying in the area or not. Tessa was convinced her mother was just too scared to commit to a decision one way or the other. As long as she was staying in Tessa's apartment, it was like she didn't have to admit that the separation from Tessa's father was becoming a permanent thing. Getting her own apartment would be like admitting that her marriage was finally

TESSA'S WINTER

over.

"Is he coming over for Christmas?" her mother asked. "We don't even have a tree yet. We should get a tree. They're selling them in that lot over by the Walmart. We can stop by this weekend."

Tessa didn't believe in cutting down live trees for Christmas. It went against everything the gardener in her stood for. She didn't much care for artificial trees, either. Last year, she and Samson had bought a little potted pine tree sapling, then after the holidays, they had given it to a friend as a gift. It was now thriving in the friend's backyard, growing the way nature intended.

"I'll ask him about it," Tessa said in a noncommittal tone. But instead, she texted Samson: *I need to get out of here. Scrabble night is driving me crazy.*

He responded a moment later: *I can drive by and pick you up. You'll have to run alongside the car and jump in...I'm not risking stopping and getting dragged into Scrabble night along with you!*

Tessa laughed, drawing frowns from everyone else at the table. Her mother cleared her throat. "It's your turn, dear."

"Oh. Right." Tessa gave a cursory glance over the board, but she had essentially given up already. She played "It" for two points, not caring at this point.

Seriously, though, she texted to Samson. *I need a night out. If I have to go home and sit through one more night of watching* How It's Made *on the Discovery channel with Mom, I'm going to lose my mind.*

I can pick you up in twenty minutes, Samson replied.

Tessa heaved a sigh of relief.

The game ended a few rounds later, with Terry pulling in the winning score when he played "Cadenza" on a Triple Word Score. Before everyone else had even finished adding up their final totals, Tessa got up, grabbed her coat, and slung her purse over her shoulder. "Well, this was fun, but I've got to get going. Samson and I are going out tonight."

"You're leaving this early?" her mother asked, checking her watch. "That's a shame. I thought we could get one more game in."

"Oh, let her go have fun," Terry said, smiling at Tessa and waving a hand for her to leave. "She's too young to be sitting in a church basement with all of us when she could be having a night out."

Tessa flashed Terry a grateful smile. She gave her mother a kiss on the cheek. "I'll see you later, Mom."

"Okay, dear." Her mother let out a heavy sigh. "I'll see you at home."

Tessa froze, wincing. That was the first time her mother had called Tessa's apartment "home." She really worried that her mother had completely forgotten that this was supposed to be a temporary arrangement.

She headed for the stairs. Before she got out of earshot, she heard her mother say to Terry, "I know she doesn't like spending time with me. But at least she could be less rude. On her phone all night!"

Tessa ground her teeth, refusing to take the bait. But she had the feeling she'd be hearing it from her mother later tonight.

It wasn't until she was standing outside the church, waiting for Samson to show up, that Tessa realized there was a big flaw in her plan. She had left her car at home, instead opting to carpool with Terry and Mrs. Mackenzie. And Samson didn't even own a car; he was determined to eliminate as much of his carbon footprint as possible, so he rode a bicycle almost everywhere, or occasionally took public transportation. Though every once in awhile he would borrow a friend's car when it was unavoidable.

No such luck today, however. A few minutes after she got outside, Samson pedaled up on his bike, flashing her a smile. Between the bike, the woven hemp pants, and the long hair that fell halfway down his back, Samson looked about as much like a hippie as anyone ever could. Though the image was a bit ruined by the ear buds he wore, which were plugged into one of the latest smartphone models. Samson might go all natural in almost everything else, from his clothes to his food to his home-brewed teas, but at least he kept in touch with some modern technological necessities.

"Madam," Samson said, bowing to her. "Your chariot awaits."

He patted the bike's handlebars.

Tessa laughed, shaking her head and taking a step back. "I'm not getting on that."

"But you have to," Samson said, nodding to the church. "If we don't make our getaway, the evil Scrabble monster is going to swallow you whole."

Tessa shook her head again, always amused by Samson's carefree attitude. "Yeah, well, Scrabble monster or no Scrabble monster, I'm not getting on your bike. That's too dangerous."

"Not at all." He took her hand and pulled her over to the bike, turning her around so she was facing front. "I've done this a million times. Trust me."

"We're gonna get hurt," Tessa said. She slung her purse diagonally across her chest, then hesitantly reached behind her for the handlebars. Samson had a pair of metal pegs attached to the center of the wheel, and she used them to step up, then she planted her butt down on the handlebars. She immediately regretted it when the bike started wobbling. "This is too dangerous. Never mind, I'm getting

TESSA'S WINTER

down."

"No, you're not," Samson said. Before she could climb back down, he pushed off, riding forward with her perched precariously on the handlebars.

"Samson! Stop!" Tessa squealed and tightened her grip on the handlebars. She felt like the bike was out of control. She tried to hold herself as still as possible, but every wobble made her feel like she was going to tip over.

"You're fine!" Samson laughed, picking up speed.

"Don't go faster!"

"Faster is safer," Samson said. "The more momentum we have, the more we'll stay centered."

The first time they went around a bend, Tessa closed her eyes tight, certain she was about to faceplant down onto the street. But Samson kept her perfectly balanced. After a couple of minutes, she actually started to relax and enjoy the ride. It was cold outside and the wind chilled her exposed skin, but other than that she found herself having a great time.

Twenty minutes later, Samson stopped in front of a little Italian restaurant a few blocks from their apartments. Tessa had driven past it hundreds of times without ever going in, and she'd mentioned it to Samson recently. Apparently he had remembered.

She got down off the handlebars, a bit wobbly after the ride. Before Samson got off the bike she pulled him close and hugged him tight. "See, that's why I love you," she said.

"Because of my excellent bike riding skills?" He smirked.

"No. Because without you, I'd never try stuff like that, and I'd have a lot less fun.

"I don't know," Samson said, chaining his bike to a street lamp, "you seem to get yourself into enough wacky situations without my help."

They headed inside and got a table. The restaurant was small and quaint, styled in a way that was half Italian diner, half Mom and Pop pizza place. The menu had the usual pizza, french fries, and wings, but there were also a lot of homemade pasta dishes that Tessa had trouble deciding between. She finally settled on a fettuccine Alfredo, which turned out to be as good as any she'd gotten at a more expensive place like Olive Garden, but at half the price.

"Mmm, see," she said between bites, "this is why I love little places like this. The food is amazing and you don't have to pay $25 per plate."

"If I ever owned my own place," Samson said, looking around, "it would be like this. Except with less pasta, more herbal teas."

Tessa arched an eyebrow. "Have you thought about opening your own place?"

Samson shrugged, pushing the food

around on his plate with his fork. "From time to time. Working at the music shop is great. I get to listen to music all day, and the customers are very chill. But the problem with working for a privately owned shop like that is there's no room for advancement. Right above me is the owner, so I can't really get promoted."

Tessa pursed her lips. "I never knew you thought about career advancement like that." Tessa worked in the corporate world, in the Quality Assurance Department at Dunham Enterprises, a nationwide organic food distributor. She had aspirations to one day moving up to head of her department, and maybe beyond that. But for all the time she'd known Samson, he had seemed content to work at the little indie music shop one of his friends owned. It was curious to see there was more to his career goals than she'd ever known.

"I don't know if I'd ever have the resources to do it," Samson said. "I'd need a good location with cheap rent. And I'd have to come up with a more well-defined product line than just my herbal teas. But I've thought about it."

It had been awhile since they'd talked about the future like this. Tessa had felt for awhile, ever since her mother moved in, that her future with Samson was on hold. She had a moment of worry that he might be thinking about his career more because the future of their relationship had stalled out. Was there still a place for her in his life if he became an entrepreneur?

They chatted for a little while longer about Samson's ideas for the cafe, which included a salad bar with homegrown produce, a variety of fresh baked goods, and a lounge area where customers could sit and read or listen to music. The more he talked about it, the more Tessa believed that this had been on Samson's mind for some time. She just wondered why he had never brought it up before.

J.L. STARR

Eventually the conversation came back around to Tessa's evening with her mother. "How is she doing?" Samson asked. "Any progress on when she'll be moving out?"

"No, actually," Tessa said, her shoulder slumping. "Today she was asking me about our plans for Christmas."

"Ouch." Samson frowned. "Do you think the holidays will make her miss your dad more? Maybe she'll head back down there, spend Christmas with him."

"I don't think so. She wants to get us a Christmas tree. And she was asking if you were going to spend Christmas with us."

A disappointed look crossed Samson's face. It made Tessa frown in concern. "What?" she asked. "Did you not want to spend Christmas together?"

"I do," Samson said. "But I was actually hoping we could take a trip together for the holidays. Just the two of us."

"Oh?"

"Well, I was waiting to bring it up," Samson said. "I was hoping we could discuss it once we knew when your mother was moving out. But a friend of mine has a timeshare up in Vermont. I was thinking we could take a trip up there, spend the holiday in the mountains. Maybe even go skiing, if I can learn how to ski." He smirked. "Or just sit in front of the fire, sipping hot cocoa. It's been a long time since we could really have that kind of alone time together."

Tessa felt a surge of guilt. Her mother's constant presence had ruined their chances to be alone together. There had been no more lazy weekend mornings sipping tea while sitting on the sofa, since her mother was sleeping on the sofa bed. There were no more romantic dinners for two, since now they had to set a table for three. And it wasn't even like they could really spend time together at Samson's place, since he was staying in his friend's basement, and that wasn't exactly the most romantic environment.

"I'd like to go," Tessa said, her voice hesitant.

"But you can't just abandon your mother at Christmas."

Tessa shrugged. "I mean, maybe we can work something out. Spend Christmas Eve with her, then drive up that night? Though she'd probably complain about waking up alone on Christmas morning."

"Well, Tessa." Samson sighed, a sympathetic look on his face. "I know you want to help take care of your mother, and I feel bad for what she's going through. But she seems to have forgotten that you have your own life now. *We* have a life together." He reached across the table and took her hand. "I'd like for us to be able to live that life together. To take the next step, like we were going to six months ago."

Tessa couldn't meet Samson's eyes. Her gut clenched in guilt. She knew Samson was right. He was voicing the same concerns she herself had been having. But she didn't know what to do about it.

"I'll talk to my mom," she said. "Maybe we can work something out."

"Well, I'll need to know about the trip by next week," Samson said. "My friend offered me the timeshare first, but if we can't take it, he's going to give it to someone else."

"Okay. I'll talk to her this weekend."

They finished the meal and headed back home. Tessa wanted to invite Samson inside, but she knew her mother was in there. She said goodbye to Samson at the front door to the apartment, then watched him get on his bike and ride away. It used to be that he'd only have to walk down the hall to get back to his place. Now he seemed so far away. No more dropping in on a whim, or working together in the gardens all afternoon. It was like the very structure of their relationship had been compromised, and she didn't know how to fix it.

She headed inside. "Mom, I'm home."

She found her mother sleeping on the couch. It wasn't even 9:00 yet.

Tessa sighed and headed into her room. It was way too early for her to go to bed yet, but she couldn't watch TV or do anything else that might make noise and disturb her mother. She booted up her computer, plugged in her headphones, and put on some music.

Then she started searching for cheap apartments for her mother. She knew her mother wasn't really ready yet. But Tessa needed her to move on. And if that meant she had to take care of it herself, then so be it.

Chapter Three

Tessa woke up the next morning to the sweet smell of something baking in the apartment. She got out of bed, drawn by the wonderful aroma, and wandered into the kitchen, still wearing nothing but her nightshirt and underwear.

She found a group of her neighbors in the kitchen, helping her mother bake Christmas cookies.

"Tessa," her mother said, shaking her head at her. "What's the matter with you? Go and put some pants on."

Tessa yelped and scurried away, trying to ignore the disapproving glares of her elderly neighbors. She grumbled to herself as she pulled on some pants, trying to remember what it was like to have her *own* apartment, with privacy and isolation and no groups of old ladies baking in her kitchen at 7:30 in the morning.

She returned to the kitchen, fully dressed, and the first thing she noticed was the *mess*. There were pans scattered all over the place, flour spilled on the kitchen counter, and empty packaging and wrappers on the table. Tessa closed her eyes for a moment and took a deep breath, telling herself not to make a big scene about it. Especially not in front of the neighbors.

"Good morning, Tessa," her mother said. "Aren't you running late for work?"

"Yeah. I just need some coffee." She squeezed her way past Mrs. Mackenzie, who was sprinkling colored sugar onto a batch of cookies, and made her way to the coffee pot. There were a few drops of coffee left in the bottom of the pot, and several empty mugs sitting nearby.

When Tessa looked in the cabinet, she found the coffee tin was all but empty, without enough grounds left for even half a cup.

"Oh, sorry Tessa," her mother said. "The girls and I made coffee. Don't worry, I'll pick up another can later today."

"Right," Tessa said, her shoulders slumped. "Sure, Mom. Okay."

Tessa went back to her room to get ready for work, resigning herself to having to pick up her coffee at the convenience store around the corner. She headed out without either coffee or breakfast, since there was no room in the kitchen for her to even put together something simple. She made do with a cup of Wawa coffee and a premade breakfast sandwich, even though she usually preferred to avoid those kinds of fatty, processed foods. It gave her a stomachache, but she powered through it, trying to keep herself focused during her long day at work.

While she was at work, Tessa couldn't stop thinking about the situation with her mother. Not only was it driving her crazy to be living with her mother, but it broke her heart to think that her parents might really be splitting up for good.

She spent some more time, during breaks in between her work, looking at potential apartments for her mother. But when she found a cute little place that looked affordable enough, all she could think about was her mother living the rest of her days in a tiny apartment, alone, with nothing to fill her time but Scrabble club and baking cookies.

There had been a time when she would have been out socializing with Tessa's dad, going on double dates together, or taking Caribbean cruises or other vacations. Her dad had a small fishing boat, and they used to go out on fishing trips together. Tessa remembered the way her mother had always been too much of a wimp to bait a hook herself, or the way she'd cooed over how cute the sand shark they'd caught was. They'd once had a great life together, and Tessa couldn't bear the thought of seeing that fall apart.

On her lunch break, she sent her dad an email. She wasn't sure how to broach the subject of him and her mother getting back together, so she approached it indirectly, asking him what his plans for Christmas were. Then she slipped in a not-so-subtle line about how "Mom and I have been discussing plans, but everything is still up in the air." She didn't know if he would get the hint—her dad could be a bit dense sometimes—but it was the only thing she could think to do.

Near the end of the day, when Tessa was finishing up one of her reports on the latest quality control tests at one of Dunham's distribution facilities, her dad called.

She sighed and picked up the phone. It was typical of her dad to call instead of emailing her back. He had said more than once in the past that talking to someone on the phone was "just easier than writing it all out." She always thought it was just an excuse he used when he was lonely and wanted to chat.

"Hi, Dad." She cradled the phone against her shoulder so she could keep typing her report while they talked. "I guess you got my email?"

"Yes, dear. I've been meaning to give you a call anyway. How is everything?"

Tessa paused in her work for a moment, trying to decide how to answer that. She didn't want to just dump her worries over her mother onto him all at once. But she needed to at least touch on the issue. "Well, things are kinda okay, I guess. Mom and I have been having a rough couple of months."

"That's a shame," he said. "How is your mother holding up? I haven't heard from her since..."

Tessa bit her lower lip. She didn't know what the best approach here was. "Well, Dad, she seems really lonely. She doesn't really have any friends up here."

She knew that was at least partially a lie. Her mother had been making friends with lots of Tessa's neighbors. But she wanted to at least generate some sympathy in her dad.

"That's too bad," her father said. "Well, I hope you two have a good holiday at least. I'll be mailing your gifts soon, so you should keep an eye out for the packages."

"I was hoping for the chance to see you for the holidays," Tessa said. "Maybe you could come up for a visit?"

Her father was silent for a long, awkward moment. "Tessa, I don't think that's such a good idea."

"But Dad—"

"Now, Tessa, I know you're upset about what's been going on between your mother and I. But frankly, I think it's unfair for you to put this on me. Your mother is the one who decided to leave."

"She only left because she said she feels like you were too distant."

"Well, that's her opinion on the matter. I don't have anything else to say about it."

"Dad, come on." Tessa leaned back in her chair, staring at the ceiling.

"I'm sorry, Tessa. But that's my final word on the subject. Besides, I've got a trip planned for the holidays, so swinging up your way wouldn't really be practical."

"A trip?" Tessa asked. "Dad, you're going on vacation without Mom?"

"Well, she's not here, now is she?" He harrumphed into the phone. "Besides, I've been wanting to take a vacation to Scotland for years now. You know my grandfather was from Scotland, and I've got some second or third cousins still living out there. Your mother never wanted to go. Said she'd rather go to Paris because it was 'more romantic.' Well, this is my life now, and I'm taking the trip I've always wanted to take."

Tessa felt like she was on the verge of tears. She had been worried for awhile about her parents being separated, but somehow, knowing her dad was taking a vacation by himself made it seem all the more real. Like he was moving on, and starting to plan his life without Tessa's mother in it. The idea that they really were splitting up was breaking Tessa's heart.

"I'm sorry if I've upset you, dear," her father said. "This is just the way things are."

"Yeah, Dad," Tessa said, her voice scratchy and hoarse. "I know."

"You take care of yourself now, dear. And take care of your mother for me."

Tessa closed her eyes, fighting off tears.

"I love you, Tessa."

J.L. STARR   383

"Love you too, Dad," Tessa said. She took a deep, shuddering breath, trying to keep herself under control.

After she got off the phone with her father, she had trouble concentrating on the rest of her work. She ended up deciding to leave work early, making an excuse to her department head and slipping out before anyone could ask her what was wrong.

When she got home, she wanted nothing more than to make a nice warm mug of tea, sit on the couch, and relax. Any other time of the year, she would have gone out to her garden and buried her sorrows in the dirt. But with the frigid weather closing in, her garden beds were nothing more than bare patches of dirt. Instead, she supposed she'd have to content herself with putting her feet up and watching Netflix.

But when she got inside, her plans, such as they were, were smashed to pieces. The couch bed was still pulled

TESSA'S WINTER

out and covered in tangled sheets and discarded clothing. The kitchen was still a mess, with the sink piled up with dishes and pans from her mother's baking adventure that morning. The garbage was piled up so high that her mother had apparently pulled out a second trash bag, filled it with the empty containers from the eggs, flour, and other ingredients, then set the bag down next to the already full can rather than emptying the trash. And on top of that, the counters and stove top had only been given a cursory wipe-down, leaving some batter stains that had dried and would now need to be scraped up.

Tessa threw her purse down on the table, clenching her teeth and holding back a scream. Her mother was nowhere to be found, but she had left a note pinned to the fridge: "Tessa—I'm working a night shift at Hallmark until 9:00. See you when I get home! P.S. Don't worry about the mess in the kitchen, I'll clean it up in the morning."

"In the morning," Tessa said, staring at the note. She ripped it off the fridge, crumpled it up, and tossed it into the trashcan, where it bounced off the pile of overflowing trash and landed on the floor.

Tessa was so on edge that she decided to do something she rarely did. She opened up the cabinet and dug out the bottle of peach schnapps she'd been saving. But when she opened the bottle, she found there was only enough left inside for maybe a shot glass.

She drank the bare mouthful of schnapps and tossed the bottle into the loose trash bag on the floor. Then she leaned against the wall and slid down to the floor, burying her face in her hands.

Tessa was tired. Tired of her parents being separated. Tired of having her life thrown into upheaval. Tired of having her own plans pushed to the back burner. And tired of feeling like she wasn't even welcome in her own home.

But most of all, she was tired of making excuses for her mother. It was time for Tessa to do something about it.

Chapter Four

Saturday morning, Tessa took her mother out with the excuse that they'd be doing some Christmas shopping. Really, though, she was determined to have a serious talk with her mother, and she wasn't going to be taking any more excuses.

They spent the first part of the day going around the mall, doing some shopping for friends and family. Tessa fretted over what to buy Samson—he was too anti-commercialism most of the time, making him hard to shop for—but eventually she settled on a set of BlueTooth speakers for his phone and a portable solar-powered phone charger. She figured that would cater both to the environmentalist in him and to the side of him that was still a hardcore techie, keeping up with the latest gadgets even while he tried to reduce his carbon footprint and stay in touch with nature.

When they swung by a sporting goods store, Tessa decided it was time to—very carefully—bring up the subject of Dad.

"What do you think Dad would like this year?" Tessa asked, looking over some fishing gear. She never knew anything much about fishing poles and such, making it hard to shop for her father. Though considering his corny sense of humor, she knew she could always go for something in the novelty singing bass genre.

"I haven't really thought about it," her mother said, avoiding eye contact while she pretended to look at some football t-shirts.

"Well, aren't you getting him anything?" Tessa asked, eyeing her mother sidelong. "I mean, I know you guys are separated, but it's Christmas, Mom."

Her mother sighed, a guilty look on her face. Which is exactly what Tessa was hoping for.

"I mean, I know he's going to be lonely on Christmas," Tessa said, looking through the shelves of novelty sporting goods. "It'll be nice if he at least has some gifts to open Christmas morning."

"Well it would have been nice if he hadn't left me feeling so lonely that I had to move out," her mother said. "But I guess sometimes we don't get what we want, do we?"

Tessa gave her mother a shocked look. She had always known her mother could have a passive aggressive side, but she hadn't been prepared for this level of spite.

She dropped the subject of Dad for the time being, trying to figure out a way to handle the situation without starting an all-out argument with her mother. They did a little more shopping, then stopped in the food court for lunch.

While they were eating, her mother asked, "So, have you talked to Samson about Christmas? I was thinking it'd be nice if we all got together for breakfast Christmas morning. I thought I'd make French toast. Oh and I thought we'd invite Gladys over, too. Most of her family is out of state, and she told me she wasn't feeling up to the drive this year, poor thing."

"Gladys?" Tessa asked, frowning in confusion.

"Gladys Mackenzie? Your neighbor?"

"Oh." Tessa blushed. She had known Mrs. Mackenzie for years, and they had shared produce from their gardens together many times, but somehow Tessa had never learned her name.

"Then later in the day," her mother said, "I thought we'd all go to mass together. It's been such a long time since we've been to Christmas mass together as a family."

Tessa chewed on the inside of her cheek. She hadn't been to mass since she moved out of her mother's house when she left for college. Religion had just never been a big part of her life, much to her mother's disappointment.

"Actually," Tessa said, looking down at her plate and pushing a French fry around in the ketchup, "Samson and I were talking about going to Vermont for Christmas."

"Vermont?" Her mother frowned at her, a look of betrayal spreading across her face. "But dear, I thought we were going to spend Christmas together?"

"Well, I thought you'd have moved back home to Florida by now."

Her mother's frown deepened. She dropped her hands down into her lap, sitting up a bit straighter. "So that's how it is, then? I came up here wanting to be with my daughter, my only real family.

Am I so much of a burden, then?"

"No, it's not that," Tessa said, trying to forget about all the times she'd come home to a messy apartment or had to cancel her plans with Samson over the last few months. "It's just...you and Dad haven't even spoken since you moved out. Don't you want to at least try to make things work? You've been married for almost thirty years. It's like that doesn't mean anything."

"I didn't come here to be lectured, Teresa May Jude. And I don't see you trying to convince your *father* to make amends. This is all his fault, after all."

Tessa closed her eyes and tilted her head back, barely holding in a groan of frustration. It had been years since her mother had called her by her full first, middle, and confirmation name. It had taken years of her high school life to get everyone around her to start calling her "Tessa" instead of "Teresa," but her mother still managed to pull the full name out whenever she was pissed off enough.

"I shouldn't be the one having to reconcile things between the two of you," Tessa said. "I'm your daughter, not your marriage counselor."

"No one *asked* you to get involved," her mother said. "I was doing just fine without you poking your nose into my business."

"You made it my business!" Tessa said, throwing her hands up in the air. "My whole life has been pushed aside because of this, so yeah, Mom, I think it's my business. I barely get to spend any time together with my boyfriend anymore. We were supposed to move in together, and now that can't happen, and we can't even take a holiday trip together because *you'd* be too lonely." She glared at her mother, feeling a bit guilty for finally letting it all out like this, but feeling justified at the same time. She'd been holding it all in for too long.

"Well," her mother said, shifting uncomfortably in her seat. "If that's how you feel about it, then maybe it's time I just went and got my own place."

Tessa felt a surge of guilt threatening her, but she pushed it away. "Fine. Maybe you should do that."

"Fine." Her mother looked away, not meeting her eye.

They ate the rest of the meal in silence. When it was done, Tessa was ready to just head straight home. But while they were carrying the shopping bags back to the car, her mother, in a terse tone of voice, asked, "Well are we at least still going to get a Christmas tree?"

Tessa sighed. The holiday spirit was really the last thing on her mind right now, but she supposed it would be petty of her to refuse to get a tree at this point. "Yeah. Sure. Okay."

They drove down to a lot, taking up

half the space of a Walmart parking lot, that sold live trees. Tessa insisted on getting a live, potted tree, so they headed down to the end of the lot to look at those. Her mother complained that they all looked smaller than the freshly cut trees, but Tessa was insistent.

While they were looking at trees, Tessa glanced over at the little strip mall that shared a parking lot with the Walmart. Something had caught her attention out of the corner of her eye, though it took her a moment to zero in on it.

A moment later she saw Samson there, standing in front of the little jewelry store on the corner of the strip mall. She was about to wave and call out to him, but then she saw that he was talking to someone. To a woman.

Tessa frowned, stepping behind a Christmas tree and peeking out at Samson from between the branches. He was too far away for her to hear what he

TESSA'S WINTER

was saying, but the woman with him was smiling and laughing. And at one point, she touched his arm, in a seemingly innocent but way too familiar fashion.

Tessa ground her teeth. She didn't want to think that there was anything going on. She trusted Samson. He wasn't the cheating type. But then again, she'd said the same thing about her father, yet that hadn't stopped her mother from getting suspicious. And Tessa had to admit that she and Samson had been growing more distant lately. A little, irrational voice in the back of her mind told her that Samson might be feeling lonely and neglected.

She was still trying to silence that voice when she saw Samson put his arms around the woman. They shared an all-too-friendly embrace. Then Samson got on his bike and rode away.

Tessa stared at him as he rode off, then she watched the woman as she headed into the jewelry shop. It looked like maybe she worked there.

Tessa shifted from one foot to the other, watching the jewelry shop. The rational side of her said there was probably a perfectly innocent explanation. But the jealous side of her wasn't listening.

"I'll be right back, Mom," she said, heading across the parking lot. "Pick out whatever tree you like."

Her mother called out to her, asking where she was going. But Tessa ignored her.

She headed straight for the jewelry shop and stepped inside. She needed to find out if there was anything going on.

Chapter Five

Tessa wandered around the jewelry shop, trying to act casual. She didn't know what she was even doing here. It had been an impulsive decision, but now that she was inside, she had no plan.

The woman Samson had been talking to was standing behind the counter at the other end of the room. When Tessa came in, the woman smiled at her and said, "Hello. Let me know if you need any help with anything."

"I'm just looking," Tessa said, trying to keep a steady tone. She didn't look directly at the woman, but she eyed the woman sidelong, trying to get a feel for who she was. She looked to be a few years younger than Tessa, and a nagging voice in her head said that the other woman was prettier than Tessa, too, with a more slender figure and a more perfect face. She wore some rather stunning jewelry, including a pair of gold and ruby earrings that sparkled in the store's dim lighting.

Tessa kept wandering around the room, looking into the glass display cases without really paying attention to the jewelry on display. There were signs in several of the display cases advertising some of the products as handmade. And she did have to admit that a lot of it was quite lovely, and it perfectly suited her own tastes— tastefully elegant without being overstated, and a lot of the pieces had nature themes, from gold pendants in the shape of leaves to diamond rings in floral motifs.

The woman behind the counter kept to herself, checking her phone while keeping an eye on Tessa. She was probably used to people coming in, looking around, then leaving without buying anything. Tessa really didn't want to buy anything, but she wanted to know who this woman was and why she'd been hugging Tessa's boyfriend.

"See anything you like?" the woman asked when Tessa wandered closer to her.

"Umm...I'm not sure," Tessa said. "It's all really lovely."

"Why, thank you." The woman wore a proud smile.

Tessa gave her a friendly smile, but avoided eye contact. She caught a glimpse of the woman's name tag and saw that her name was Tori. She didn't remember Samson ever talking about a Tori before. She knew it was possible she was just being paranoid. That Samson had simply been here as a customer. But Samson had never bought her jewelry before. It wasn't really his style. For her last birthday he'd gotten her a painting done by a local artist, and for Christmas the year before he'd gotten her a hand-woven floral patterned rug. The idea of Samson buying her one of these gold necklaces, lovely as they were, just seemed out of character for him.

Tessa finally convinced herself she was being foolish, and she headed for the door. "Thanks," she said, giving the woman a polite smile.

"Have a nice day," Tori said. She returned her attention to her phone before Tessa even got out the door.

Tessa stepped outside and leaned against the wall, letting out a slow breath. She told herself she was just being paranoid. That the problems her parents had been going through were making her jump to the wrong conclusions. And she'd gotten herself into plenty of trouble in the past by jumping to conclusions instead of just asking questions. Though she didn't see how she could just ask Samson what he had been doing here without making it seem like she was suspicious of him.

She headed back to the tree lot. Her mother had picked out a tree, and they arranged to have it delivered to Tessa's apartment, since tying it to the roof of the car wasn't so practical with a potted plant, and there wasn't enough room for it in the car.

"Find anything interesting?" her mother asked as they got in the car.

"What?"

Her mother nodded towards the jewelry store. "In that little shop there. Did you find anything nice?"

"Oh. No." Tessa frowned and shook her head. She certainly wasn't about to tell her mother about her suspicions.

They went home and spent the next couple of hours wrapping Christmas presents and hanging decorations, while the tension from their earlier argument still hung in the air between them. And the entire time, Tessa kept thinking about Samson and the jewelry store girl. Eventually, when her mother went to lie down for a nap, Tessa decided that she couldn't take the mystery any more. She decided to Google the girl.

It didn't take long to find some results. Plugging the jewelry store's name into the search engine brought up a LinkedIn profile for a Victoria Oliver. The picture matched the girl Tessa had seen at the shop. According to the profile, she was the shop's owner, and she apparently made most of the jewelry herself. That almost made Tessa feel a little bit better—she knew that if Samson was going to go shopping anywhere, it would be at a local indie store where everything was handmade. But it still didn't explain whether he was there shopping for Tessa for Christmas or if there was something else going on.

She decided to do a bit more searching for the name Victoria Oliver, and that's when she found something that made her stomach churn.

She found Victoria's Facebook page, and after looking around for a bit, she found a lot of mutual friends between Victoria and Samson. Worse yet, when she dug through Victoria's pictures, she found some old photos, dating back to a few years ago, that showed Samson and her together. The pictures were taken at a variety of places, from Samson's music shop, to the beach down in Wildwood, to the Pennsylvania Renaissance Fair.

And in quite a few of the pictures, Samson and Victoria were hugging, kissing, and generally looking like a happy couple.

Once she'd dug through the pictures, Tessa remembered: Samson had, from time to time, mentioned an old girlfriend, "Vicky." It seemed that either somewhere along the way, Victoria had changed from Vicky to Tori, or that Vicky had just been Samson's pet name for her. Either way, this was the same woman.

She couldn't remember much of what Samson had said about his ex. Only that they'd started off as friends in school, then things had gotten serious for awhile, but they'd eventually broken up. They'd parted on good terms, but Tessa hadn't ever thought that meant Samson was still in touch with the woman. She had no idea if they still saw each other on a regular basis, or if their encounter at the jewelry store had been a one time thing. Maybe, she told herself, Samson had simply bumped into his ex while he was out shopping, and they'd spent some time chatting and reminiscing. Maybe it was just innocent. Maybe.

She thought about just asking him directly. But she was afraid. Afraid of what she might find out, and afraid that Samson would get upset if she turned out to be accusing him of something he was innocent of. So after spending most of the afternoon thinking about it, she came up with a plan.

A plan that would, hopefully, help ease her worries without ever letting Samson know that she had doubted him.

Chapter Six

That night, Tessa dropped in on Samson unannounced. It felt a bit strange to be doing so. Before her mother had moved in, they had both gotten so used to dropping in on each other that it had almost been as if their two apartments, right down the hall from each other, were just different rooms in the same house. Half the time, Tessa hadn't even locked her door during the day, leaving Samson free to swing by any time he felt like strolling down the hall.

Now that he was living on the other side of town, dropping in on him felt more like an intrusion. But she did it anyway, driving over to the house he was staying at and walking around the back to the basement door. She walked down the short flight of steps to the basement door and knocked.

"Just a moment," Samson called out from inside. She heard some slight rustling, then a moment later, Samson opened the door.

"Tessa," he said, grinning happily. "I thought you were spending the day shopping with your mother."

"I was," she said. "But, well, I guess I couldn't handle being around her for one more minute." That was partially true, though she knew it wasn't the real reason she was here.

Samson let her in and offered to make some tea. The basement had a little kitchenette installed in one corner, and Samson started a pot of water boiling on the mini stove. They chatted a bit about the holiday shopping they'd been doing, and Tessa spent some time griping about the argument she'd had with her mother. Though she carefully avoided mentioning the way she'd seen Samson at the jewelry store.

"Any word on Christmas?" Samson asked. "I don't suppose she's decided to move out yet?"

"Well, after the fight we had today, she might be." Tessa sighed, flopping down on the couch. Samson's keys and wallet were sitting on the end table right next to her. She eyed them sidelong, trying to pretend that she wasn't up to anything.

"Did you tell her about Vermont?"

"Yeah. She didn't seem happy about it. I don't know what to do."

"Well, we need to make up our minds soon," Samson said. "I need to let my friend know whether we're taking the place."

"I know." Tessa leaned back against the couch, staring at the ceiling. "I'll talk to her again when I get home, and get a definite answer."

Samson brought her a mug of tea. "I wish we didn't have to deal with all of this stress around the holidays," he said. "You know I hate drama around Christmas. Almost as much as I hate the commercialism."

"I know." Tessa smiled up at him. His practical nature was one of the things she loved about him. And looking up at him, seeing the smile on his face and the love in his eyes, she wondered how she could ever have doubted him.

Though when he excused himself to go to the bathroom, she knew she still had to snoop a little. She grabbed his wallet and looked inside, sorting through the messy little stack of receipts he had tucked into one of the wallet's compartments. She found one that was handwritten in a neat, flowing script. The receipt didn't list the shop's name— it was from one of those generic receipt paper pads that small business owners could buy at Staples or Walmart—but the description on the receipt was a dead giveaway: "(1) Gold/Custom/Engraved."

Tessa's heart fluttered. The receipt seemed to confirm what the more sensible side of her had been saying all along. He had simply been there shopping for jewelry. Which suddenly made her feel guilty as heck. Not only because she'd been snooping, but also because she'd apparently just ruined the surprise of her Christmas gift. Though the receipt didn't say whether it was a necklace, earrings, or a bracelet, so maybe there would still be some surprise left. And she had to admit, the jewelry in Tori's little shop had certainly been stunning.

She quickly tucked the receipt away, and tried her best to act innocent when Samson returned from the bathroom.

They spent the rest of the evening together, and if Samson noticed the tension Tessa was still carrying with her, he didn't say anything about it. For her part, she kept a brave face on, refusing to let herself ruin the evening by talking about her stupid suspicions and paranoia.

They had dinner and spent some time discussing the possible Vermont trip, including tentative plans to drive over to New Hampshire one day in order to drive to the top of Mount Washington. Tessa had been there once when she was a teenager, and she had always wanted to visit it again, even if she did have some problems with heights.

After dinner with Samson, Tessa headed home to talk to her mother about the difficult subject of her moving out. When she got there, she found her mother already looking through the newspaper—an actual old-fashioned paper newspaper—searching the classifieds for apartment listings.

"It'd be easier if you do that online," Tessa said.

"No thank you," her mother said,

raising her chin and refusing to make eye contact. "I prefer to do things my own way."

Tessa sighed. Her mother wasn't completely technologically illiterate, but she did tend to be stuck in the past.

Tessa kept herself busy for a little while, using her laptop to look up sights to see in Vermont, while trying to decide how best to start talking to her mother without starting another argument. Her mother kept checking the classifieds and making a few phone calls to the apartments she was looking at. Eventually, it was her mother who broke the silence.

"Well, I have some bad news for you, dear."

"What's wrong?" Tessa asked.

"Well, there's plenty of apartments in my price range. None too close to here, really, but I don't mind a bit of a drive. But none of them are going to be available before January."

"That's fine," Tessa said, shrugging it off. She could handle another few weeks with her mother, despite the problems they'd been having.

"Well, I know you wanted me out of the way before Christmas."

Tessa let out a frustrated groan, burying her face in her hands. "Why do you have to do that?"

"Do what, dear?" her mother asked. "I'm just going by what you said."

Tessa shook her hands at her mother, almost ready to strangle her. "I never said I wanted you out of the way. And I didn't say you had to leave by Christmas."

Her mother looked away, folding her hands in her lap. "Well, you aren't going to be here for Christmas. And I certainly don't want to be sitting in this apartment all by myself on the holiday while you and your boyfriend run off to Vermont."

Tessa rubbed her hands across her

face. She hated it when her mother acted like this. She wanted to ask her mother what would be so different about moving out before Christmas and sitting alone in her own apartment, instead of sitting alone in Tessa's. But it was a losing argument, and she knew it.

There was just no way her mother was going to let this go. Tessa hated having to compromise like this, but she knew if she wanted to clear this situation up and make her mother happy, she was going to have to give in.

"Well," Tessa said, her voice filled with resignation, "I don't think Samson and I are taking that trip, anyway."

"You're not?" Her mother finally looked at her, a hopeful look in her eyes.

Tessa quickly spun a lie in her head. She would never admit, at least not directly, that the real reason she was canceling the trip was to get her mother to stop guilt tripping her. "I don't think I can take the time off work, really. I only get the three-day weekend off, but if I wait until after the new year, then my vacation hours at work reset and I can take off a full week. So we might push the trip back until Valentine's."

"Oh, well wouldn't that be romantic." He mother smiled wide. It almost looked like a triumphant grin. "And that means Samson can come over here to spend Christmas with us. And with Gladys."

"Yeah," Tessa said, turning back to her computer screen without really focusing on it. Her gaze drifted off, distant, as she reconciled herself to yet another one of her big plans being pushed back, delayed indefinitely, because of her mother. "Yeah, it'll be great."

Chapter Seven

Over the next few weeks, Tessa finally started to feel like things were settling into a sort of equilibrium. There was still some tension with her mother, but it was reduced by the knowledge that one way or the other, her mother would be moving out soon. She could deal with the occasional sink full of dishes, or the way she'd completely lost her living room since her mother started nesting there, as long as she knew there was a definite time limit on how long it would go on. New Year's Day became a big deadline that she clung to like a life preserver, helping her to keep from drowning under the burden of living with her mother.

As Christmas approached, Tessa helped her mother bake Christmas cookies to share with the neighbors. It helped rekindle some of the communal feeling Tessa missed from the spring and summer, when she would grow vegetables in her garden to share with the community.

Making cookies from scratch had almost that same feeling of doing something with your hands and putting your time and love into it. Plus every once in awhile it was nice to let go of her sensible diet and eat something sugary for a change.

On Christmas Day, Tessa woke to the smell of French toast cooking in the apartment. She headed to the kitchen, this time stopping to make sure she had pants on first, and found her mother making breakfast. Terry Jones and Gladys Mackenzie were both there; Tessa and her mother had invited them to spend Christmas together since neither of them had anyplace else to go.

"Good morning, Tessa," her mother said, serving her up a plate of French toast. "Merry Christmas."

"Merry Christmas," Tessa said. She sat and joined Terry and Gladys at the table, and they had a nice, quiet breakfast together. On some level, Tessa missed the type of Christmas morning she'd once had as a kid, waking up to a pile of presents under the tree, eager to open them. But until she had kids of her own, that kind of magic simply wasn't a part of Christmas anymore. Though she could still enjoy the quiet of a simple Christmas among friends and neighbors.

After breakfast, they sat down to watch some Christmas movies together while they chatted and sipped hot cocoa. A few gifts were exchanged, mostly small, personal tokens. Gladys gave Tessa a hand-knitted sweater, and Terry gave her a collection of seed packets she could use in her spring planting. Her mother gave her a throw pillow with a handmade cross stitch design she'd made herself, along with some new clothes and a new winter jacket.

Tessa's real excitement, of course, was for Samson's gift. He arrived in time for lunch, carrying a small stack of presents. "Merry Christmas, everyone," he said, setting the packages down and giving each of them a hug.

Tessa eyed the packages. Each of them was fairly large—large enough to hold books or clothes, not jewelry. A slight frown touched her face, but she tried not to let herself overreact.

Samson made a show of handing out his gifts, and just as Tessa expected, there was a story behind each one. "I found that in an old antique shop down in Mullica Hill," he said as Terry opened his gift. "It was a bit scuffed and needed some repairs, but I gave it a tune up and a new layer of polish."

Terry smiled proudly as he pulled a

small antique wooden clock from the box. "It's beautiful," he said, turning it over in his hands and examining every angle. "Did I ever tell you how I used to work in the wood shop while I was in prison? Passed a lot of time working with my hands, though back then it was mostly office furniture for the prison staff."

"I remember," Samson said, patting Terry's knee. "I almost bought you a table saw so you could set up a workshop in your apartment, but I didn't think the landlord would be too keen on that."

Terry chuckled. "Oh, no, I imagine not."

He gave Gladys an old-fashioned tea set in white porcelain in a floral print pattern. "There's a few chips here and there," Samson said, holding up one of the cups. "But when I saw it, I thought that just gave it personality. A little sign of the history it's seen."

"It's lovely, Samson," Gladys said. "Thank you so much."

Samson's gift to Tessa's mother was a handmade quilt. She raved about it, saying it was just like one that had belonged to her grandmother. "You remember the one, Tessa," she said, stroking the soft fabric. "It used to hang over the back of your grandmother's sofa in the den."

Tessa gave Samson a proud smile. She didn't know how he always managed to pick out just the right thing. He seemed to have a sense for what would touch people closest to their hearts.

Last, he gave Tessa her gift. She had to fight off a frown when she saw the box. It was quite large. Far too large to be jewelry. She had been expecting him to pull another, smaller package out of his coat pocket.

"What is it?" she asked, trying to keep a serene expression on her face.

"Open it," Samson said, a big grin on

his face.

She held her breath when opening the package. Inside was a colorful winter jacket with a flared waist, decorated in a pattern of interwoven vines and autumn leaves. It was quite lovely, and Tessa would have been ecstatic over it, except that she knew for a fact that Samson had bought something from a jewelry store.

"Do you like it?" he asked.

"Yes. It's beautiful." She knew she didn't sound as excited as she should be, but she couldn't help it. She started looking the jacket over, slipping her hands into the pockets to see if there was anything inside. She found nothing.

"I noticed your old coat was a bit bulky on our bike ride a couple of weeks ago," Samson said. "This is a lot more streamlined."

Tessa forced a polite laugh. "Yeah, well, I suppose that'll help if you ever convince me to ride on your handlebars again."

"That reminds me," Samson said, snapping his fingers, a thoughtful look on his face. "I got you something else, too."

Tessa's eyebrows shot up. "Oh?"

"Come on, it's outside." He took her hands and helped her to her feet.

Tessa frowned while she followed him to the door. Had he left the jewelry outside? She gave a helpless look to her mother, but she couldn't ask her for advice about this.

They stepped out into the hall. Samson took a step to the side, spreading his arms and gesturing to a brand new bicycle. Tessa looked at the bike in confusion, then looked up at Samson, waiting for an explanation.

"So we can ride together," Samson said. "I know you aren't going to ride everywhere like I do, but I thought it would be nice if we could ride together some places. Especially when the weather gets nicer."

J.L. STARR   425

"Yeah," Tessa said, keeping a force smile on her face. "Yeah, that'd be great. I mean, in the spring it'll be great."

She gave him a hug, closing her eyes as she fought off tears. She knew there had to be another explanation. Maybe the jewelry he'd bought was for her birthday...five months away. Or for Valentine's Day. But she couldn't help the nagging feeling that there was something much worse going on here.

What if Samson, after being pushed away so much ever since Tessa's mother moved in, had bought the jewelry for another woman?

Chapter Eight

The week after Christmas, Tessa mostly kept to herself. Her mother was busy packing her things, getting ready to move into her new apartment on January 1st.

Tessa knew she should have been making plans with Samson, so they could celebrate the newfound privacy they'd have once he could move in the way they'd originally planned. But fear over the possibility of there being another woman kept hounding Tessa, and she couldn't even bring herself to pick up the phone and call Samson. When he called, she made excuses, claiming she was busy with work or with helping her mother pack. But she sensed disappointment in his tone, and she got the feeling he knew there was something going on.

Tessa came home from work one night, right before New Year's, and found her mother cleaning up the kitchen. Not just cleaning it. Scrubbing it from floor to ceiling. The stove was so pristine Tessa could almost see her reflection in it. The walls had been scrubbed so thoroughly that Tessa was astonished to learn they were actually white, not the off-tan color she'd seen for years. And the whole fridge had been emptied, scrubbed down, then reorganized. Everything was cleaner than it had been since her mother had moved in. Hell, since Tessa had first started living there.

"Oh, hello dear," her mother said, smiling at her while she continued scrubbing the stains off the inside of the microwave. "How was work?"

"It was fine," Tessa said, looking

around at the clean kitchen, not sure how to react to it. "Is this guilt?"

"What's that?" her mother asked, frowning at her.

"Guilt? Is that why you're cleaning all of a sudden?"

Her mother frowned deeper, putting her hands on her hips. "Well, I never. Tessa, I'm moving out in a couple of days. I just wanted to do something nice for you, and this is the thanks I get?"

"Okay, okay, I'm sorry." Tessa tossed her purse on the table and slumped into chair, folding her arms on the table and burying her face in her arms.

"What's wrong, dear?" her mother asked. She set aside her scrubbing pad and sat down across from Tessa.

"I don't want to talk about it.

"Is this about you and Samson? I've noticed he's barely been over lately, especially since Christmas. Did you two have a fight?"

"We've just been busy," Tessa said,

though she knew she was lying to herself as much as to her mother. She didn't want to admit the real reasons she had been avoiding Samson.

Her mother folded her hands on the tabletop. "Well, your father and I were 'too busy' for each other for a long time. Look where that got us."

Tessa sighed, leaning back in her chair. "I'm sorry, Mom, but I don't think I want relationship advice from you. Especially not when you won't even call Dad up to talk about things."

Her mother harrumphed. "Well, if that's how you're going to be..." She got up and turned back to her cleaning.

"No, Mom, wait." Tessa groaned in frustration. "I just..."

"Just what, dear?"

"I just don't want the same thing that happened to you and Dad to happen with me and Samson. Growing distant. Accusing him of cheating. Being so suspicious and closed off. How can you live like that?"

"Well, it's not like we started off that way," her mother said. "I just...I guess for a long time now, I've felt like I needed to get out there and live my own life."

"What about the life you chose with Dad?"

Her mother held a sponge in her hand, looking at the stained microwave. "It takes two people to make a life like that work. And once I felt like your father wasn't invested in it anymore, I had a choice. I could either carry the whole relationship by myself, or I could leave. And I left."

"And has that made you happy?"

Her mother didn't look at her. She stood there and stared. Her back was to Tessa, but Tessa was pretty sure her mother was fighting off tears.

"I don't suppose it has," her mother said, her voice strained. "Not that I don't like spending so much time with you lately, dear. But since moving up here I've...I've felt somehow more alone. I've made some friends, sure. But I guess that's not the same as having someone to spend your life with."

"So why don't you talk to Dad?"

Her mother shook her head. She started scrubbing the microwave again, with renewed determination. "I told you, dear. I can't be the only one carrying the relationship."

Tessa stared at her mother's back for a few minutes, then she got up and went into her bedroom, shutting the door behind her.

She didn't want her relationship with Samson to end up going down that same path. But she had to wonder if she was doing the same thing her father was doing. Letting the relationship slowly die because she was too stubborn or too afraid to go do something about it.

She picked up the phone, letting out a long sigh. She couldn't avoid talking to

Samson forever, regardless of what her fears were. She'd just have to call him and talk things out.

And she hoped that when she brought up her suspicions, they would prove to be unfounded, and that he would forgive her for overreacting.

Chapter Nine

Samson answered the phone. "Hey, honey. What's up?"

Tessa hesitated. She wasn't sure what to say or how to approach this. "Hi. Can we talk?"

"Sure. Is something wrong?"

Tessa chewed on her lower lip. She didn't want to say that things were *wrong,* per say. There was a chance that there was nothing wrong at all. That it was all in her head. "I don't know," she said. "I guess...I guess I've just been having a rough week."

"I know it must be stressful. With your Mom and Dad and that whole situation."

"Yeah." Tessa stared at the wall, not

sure what to say. Now that she had Samson on the phone, she couldn't bring herself to just outright accuse him of something.

"Tessa?"

"Yes?"

"Is there something else the matter? You seem...I don't know. Not like yourself."

"I guess I've just been spending a lot of time thinking about the future lately."

"Me too," Samson said.

"Really?"

"Yeah. I've been thinking that it's time to make some changes in my life."

Tessa's heart started to race. The dreaded voice in the back of her head told her that the "changes" he was talking about would mean leaving her behind.

"What kind of changes?" she asked.

"Well, that's not really something to talk about over the phone."

Tessa frowned, trying to puzzle out

Samson's tone of voice. He seemed hesitant, but she couldn't tell if it was because there was something he was afraid to tell her, or if he was just being playful.

"Can you just tell me now?" she asked. "You know I hate surprises."

"How about tomorrow night?" Samson said. "It's New Year's Eve. I thought we'd go out. There's this new place downtown. Brand new, actually. I'd like you to see it."

"What kind of place?"

"You'll see," Samson said. "Trust me."

A small smile touched Tessa's lips, despite her worries. She always had trusted Samson. She was ashamed of herself for even beginning to doubt him. Though the question about what he'd really been doing at the jewelry store still nagged at her mind.

"Tomorrow night," she agreed.

They set a time, and Samson promised to come pick her up at her apartment. Tessa hung up, letting out a long sigh. She told herself that it would be easier to ask what she needed to ask if she did it in person. She just hoped that it would actually be true.

Tessa was a bundle of nerves for the rest of the night and through most of the next morning. She had the day off, and in order to cope with her nerves she spent most of the morning helping her mother finish with her packing and with cleaning the rest of the apartment. They pulled the sofa bed out and vacuumed behind it, they dusted every piece of furniture in the apartment, and Tessa even pulled the bookshelves away from the walls so she could wash the walls and clean up the layers of dust that had collected on the baseboards.

She was still working on moving all the furniture back into place when there was a knock on her door. She frowned, wondering who would be dropping by on New Year's Eve of all days. Samson wouldn't have knocked.

Tessa opened the door and found her father standing there.

"Dad." She stared at him, holding the door open, unable to think. She hadn't seen her father in person since before the whole fiasco between him and her mother had started. He had barely even been returning her phone calls lately.

"Hey there, Tessa dear," he said, giving her an awkward smile. He stood there with his hands in his pockets, rocking back and forth slightly on the balls of his feet. "Is your mother here?"

Tessa's mother stepped into the room, holding a rag in one hand and a can of furniture polish in the other. "David?"

He smiled at her. "Carol. It's good to see you."

Tessa stepped to the side so her dad could come in. "I thought you were in Scotland," she said.

"I was," he said. "Ended the trip early. I wasn't having a very good time out there, all by myself."

Tessa's mother just stared at him, a dumbfounded look on her face. Her father stepped forward, giving her mother a bashful smile. "How've you been?" he asked.

Tessa's mother stood up a bit straighter, seeming to snap out of her initial shock. She turned away, setting the rag and furniture polish down on the table. "I'm doing just fine," she said, raising her chin. "Just cleaning things up here so I'll be ready to move out tomorrow. I've got my own apartment waiting for me. Already signed the lease and everything.

Tessa's father scratched the back of his head. "That's the thing," he said. "I had a lot of time to think while I was in Scotland. Lots of lonely time, really, staring into a beer."

"You always did drink too much," Mom said, not looking at him.

"Well, when you're all alone,

thousands of miles from the people you love, there's a lot of comfort in a mug of beer. And after sitting in the same bar for days on end, I decided it was time to come home. And I want you to come home, Carol."

Tessa's mother kept her back to him, keeping her hands busy by folding and refolding some rags on the table. "I've told you, David, I have a new home now. Things are going just fine for me up here. I don't need you coming back now, after six months, thinking I'll just change my mind. You can't just say you're sorry and expect that it'll make everything all right again. Besides which, you haven't actually *said* you're sorry."

"Well I am," Dad said.

"That's not good enough!" Mom threw the rags down on the table. They scattered across the tabletop, knocking over the spray can of polish. She spun to face him, clenching her fists at her sides.

"I've been working on making a new life for myself, David. A life that you haven't been any part of. And now you want me to come back to you, why, because you're lonely? Well I was lonely for *years*, David. For years. And you never seemed to care!"

"Carol..." Dad held his hands out to either side, sighing.

"Don't!" Mom took a step back, holding a finger up. "Don't you dare. I don't want to hear it." She pointed to the door. "I think you should leave."

"Mom," Tessa said, rolling her eyes. "Come on, don't be like that. Didn't you keep saying how you wanted Dad to come back? Well, he's here now." Tessa gestured to her father. "Can't you at least give him a chance?"

"This isn't your decision, Tessa," Mom said. She looked at Tessa's father. "David, please leave."

Tessa crossed her arms. "First of all," she said, "you're my parents, so I'm a part of this. And also, in case you forgot, this *is* my apartment. And I don't want Dad to leave."

Her mother scowled at her, a look of pure betrayal on her face. "Fine," Mom said, grabbing her purse. "Then I'll leave."

She headed for the door. Tessa followed her. "Mom, don't do this. Where are you even going to go? Your apartment isn't ready until tomorrow."

"I'll stay at a hotel," Mom said, opening the door. "I'll be back for my things tomorrow."

"Carol," Dad said, pleading with her but making no move to stop her. "Please, don't go."

Tessa's mother left, slamming the door shut behind her. Tessa stared at the closed door, running her hands through her hair. It took all the restraint she had not to start pulling her hair put by the roots.

Her father hung his head. "I didn't

think it would be like this," he said. "I thought I could come by, talk to her, make things right." He held up his hands for a moment, then let them drop helplessly to his sides.

Tessa sighed. She rubbed a hand over her face. "I'll talk to her," she said. "I'll figure something out."

"Maybe you shouldn't bother," Dad said, sinking down into a chair. "Maybe she was right all along."

"Please don't say that." Tessa crouched by her father's side, taking his hands in hers. "You guys have been married for such a long time. I don't want to see that fall apart. There's not even any reason. People don't just split up for no reason."

He shrugged. There was a defeated look on his face. "Sometimes, after a few decades of marriage, just being tired of each other is reason enough."

Tessa glowered at him. "Now I don't believe that for a minute. Are you really saying you're tired of Mom?"

"No." Dad sighed, shaking his head. "No, I'm not. But it seems like she is. And maybe I'm too tired of chasing her."

Tessa got up and stalked across the room. She started pacing. "That's baloney and you know it. I'm not going to let you both just give up like this. It's not like you've done anything horrible. It's not like you've cheated on each other." She gave her father an uncertain look. "Have you?"

"No! Of course not." He looked offended at the very suggestion. "I've never strayed, not in all these years. Oh, sure, I'll take a look when a girl with a nice—"

"*I don't* need to hear that from my father!" Tessa said, holding her hands out to stop him.

He smiled bashfully and shrugged. "Well, the point is, it's always been 'look, don't touch.' I'd never stray. Not that your mother seems to care about that."

Tessa sighed, burying her face in her hands. She'd dealt with this same passive aggressive attitude from her mother for six months. She wasn't going to take it from her father.

She sat down, feeling worn out. She didn't know what to do next. She needed to talk to her mother, but it would probably be best to wait until Mom had a chance to cool down. And she couldn't deal with her father right now, not when he was putting her through the same crap her mother had put her through for months. She needed to get away for a bit.

She got up and grabbed her jacket. The new one Samson had gotten her. Looking at it brought tears to her eyes, but she fought them off.

"Where are you going?" Dad asked.

"Out. I need to clear my head."

He stood up, sticking his hands in his pockets. "What am I supposed to do?"

Tessa sighed. "You can stay here if you

J.L. STARR

445

want. There's food in the fridge. And coffee in the cabinet. Just don't make a mess."

She opened the drawer in the table by the door and pulled out her spare set of keys, handing them to her father so he could come and go without being stuck alone in the apartment. Then she headed out, heading to her car without any real idea of where she was going or what she was doing.

She had driven halfway to Samson's place before she even realized that's where she was going. When she got there, she headed around the back and down the stairs to the basement door. She knocked, and by the time Samson answered the door, she was already breaking down in tears.

Chapter Ten

"What happened?" Samson asked, putting his arms around her. He led her inside and sat her down on the couch, then went to make her a cup of tea. It took Tessa a few minutes of sniveling and hiccuping before she got herself composed. The soothing aroma of the tea helped.

When she started to relax again, Tessa scrubbed the tears from her eyes. "What is this?" she asked, lifting the tea mug. The scent of the tea was something new, sweet and strong and invigorating.

"A new recipe I've been working on," Samson said with a smile. "I've been experimenting a lot lately. With tea, and with baking, too. I'll have to show you one of my new recipes when we get the chance. As it turns out," he sat up a bit straighter, wearing a proud grin, "I can make *quite* the blueberry scone."

Tessa laughed, shaking her head. She didn't know how Samson did that. She had come over here having a breakdown, and within a few minutes he had her relaxed. And hungry.

"So, did something happen between you and your mother?" Samson asked, squeezing her knee.

"Yeah. Well, her and my dad."

"Oh?" Samson leaned back on the couch, a curious expression on his face.

"Well, Dad dropped by, all of a sudden."

"I thought he was in Scotland."

"So did I," Tessa said. "Turns out, he came back early."

She told Samson about the argument her parents had gotten into, and how she'd been caught right in the middle of it. By the time she finished the story, her tea cup was empty, and her stomach was grumbling.

Samson listened thoughtfully to the story. When she was done, he pursed his lips, tapping his palms against his knees as he thought it over. Finally, he asked, "So, what are you going to do?"

She shrugged. "I really have no idea. I don't think Dad is going to go home without trying to work things out, but Mom probably won't want to talk to him. I need to figure out a way to get them into the same room without an argument starting."

Samson smirked. "Do I smell a zany scheme developing?"

Tessa laughed, shaking her head. "No. No zany schemes this time. While it would be tempting to pull some classic romantic comedy hijinks and arrange for them to 'coincidentally' end up at the same romantic candlelit dinner on the beach without realizing it, I don't think a big romantic gesture is going to be enough. They've been drifting apart for so long, I don't think one romantic moment will fix it."

"Then what will?"

"I don't know." Tessa leaned her head against Samson's shoulder. "Honestly, I think they need counseling or something. But I don't know if they're even willing to put that much effort into making it work. I need to convince them that their marriage is worth saving before they'll work to save it."

"Well," Samson said, taking one of her hands and holding it between both of his, "I'd wager that they both need some time to cool off and think things over. Which means we have the night to ourselves. Remember, I wanted to take us out to that new place in town tonight."

Tessa leaned back on the couch, covering her eyes with one hand. "Oh, God. I forgot."

"You still want to go, right?" Samson

asked.

Tessa lowered her hand and looked at him, pouting in what she hoped was an adorable enough way that he'd forgive her. "Can I take a rain check? I've got my dad sitting alone in my apartment right now, and my mom checked herself into a hotel. I need to go deal with this before it gets any worse. Besides, I don't think I could focus on having a good time when I know the two of them are so miserable."

Samson let her hand go. He leaned back, looking away from her. "If that's what you need to do."

A surge of guilt and worry passed through Tessa. She hated abandoning Samson when he had something romantic planned, especially since it felt like she was doing the same thing to him that her dad had done to her mom. And at the same time, she had to wonder if this was exactly the sort of thing that might make him start to stray. He looked so dejected, and she knew it was her fault.

"Samson, please," she said. "This is important."

"Yeah," he said, still not looking at her. "I know."

She frowned at him. "Don't be like that."

"Don't be like what?"

"You're being passive aggressive. I really don't appreciate that, not with everything I'm going through right now."

"I'm not trying to be." He looked at her without quite meeting her eye. "But it seems like this keeps happening."

"What does?"

"You having to push me aside because of something else in your life."

He got up and walked across the room, leaning against the counter in the little kitchenette and staring up at the window overhead.

"That's not fair," Tessa said. She got

TESSA'S WINTER

up and stood behind him, crossing her arms.

"I know," Samson said, hanging his head. "I didn't mean to say it."

"But obviously you were thinking it."

He shrugged.

"Samson, this isn't fair."

"Well then, maybe you should just go home for now."

Tessa felt like she'd just been slapped in the face. She swallowed a lump in her throat. "Is that really what you want?"

He still didn't look at her. "What I want...what I wanted was to make this a special night. But you want to put it off, so there we go."

Tessa shook her head. She walked over to the door and opened it, then hesitated before walking outside. "You know," she said, "you're not perfect in this relationship, either."

"What have I done?" Samson asked, turning on her with an angry glare. "Are you mad because I'm upset about our night being ruined? Am I not allowed to be upset?"

"I guess it depends on what you do when you're upset."

"What is that supposed to mean?"

Tessa looked away from him. She felt tears rolling down her cheeks. "It means I saw you the other day. At the jewelry store. With your *ex*."

"Tessa..."

"Don't," Tessa said. "Don't even bother. I know you were there, and I know what you bought there."

"You do?" Samson's eyes widened and his face went pale.

"Yup." A sneer touched Tessa's lip. "A gold, engraved necklace that was *not* my Christmas gift. I hope whoever you gave it to is very happy."

"Tessa, wait. That's not—"

"Just save it," Tessa said. She headed out the door, slamming it shut behind her.

Samson opened the door a moment

later, but she was already at the top of the stairs. "Tessa, hold on a second! Let me explain."

She ignored his words. Maybe she wasn't being fair to him. She knew that. But she was angry, and the situation with her parents had frustrated her to no end. She didn't have the patience to deal with anything else today. Not from Samson, not from her parents, not from anyone.

She hurried to her car and got inside before Samson could catch up to her. She started driving. A moment later, she saw him in the rear view mirror, following her on his bike.

She hit the accelerator and drove away, leaving him behind.

J.L. STARR

Chapter Eleven

Tessa pulled into the parking lot of her apartment complex, then immediately realized this was the last place she wanted to be.

She sat there staring at the apartment building. Her dad was inside, but she didn't want to deal with him. And there was a good chance Samson was on his way over there right that minute, and she didn't want to deal with him, either. And that was on top of the chance that her mother might come back to pick up her things.

She sat in the car for a few minutes with the engine still running. Her tears had dried up, but she was still sniffling and her nose was stuffed up. She took a few deep breaths, trying to calm herself enough to figure out what she needed to do.

Then a knock on her window made her jump in her seat and yelp.

Her neighbor, Terry Jones, stood by the car door with a concerned look on his weathered face. She rolled down the window, taking a deep breath to calm her frazzled nerves. "Terry. You scared the heck out of me."

"Sorry about that, Tessa. I just saw you sitting here and I thought maybe something was wrong. Are you okay?"

"Not...not really."

"Is there anything I can do to help?" he asked.

Tessa thought about that for a moment. "I...I don't really know. Everything is just so messed up right now."

"Why don't you come inside and talk about it?" Terry said, gesturing to the building.

Tessa looked at the apartment building, remembering that it was likely Samson was still following her on his bike. She shook her head.

"How about I buy you a drink?" she suggested.

A short time later she was sitting with Terry in a small, quiet bar a few blocks from home. The place was decorated for New Year's, but it was still early enough that it wasn't crowded yet. Surely, Tessa thought, the place would be packed later tonight, as people drank their way into the new year. She was getting a head start with a strawberry daiquiri. Terry sat across from her, nursing a glass of scotch.

"Well now, Tessa," Terry said, "we've known each other for a couple of years now, and I don't think I've ever seen you desperate to go out and have a drink. There must be something pretty major going on."

"I'm not sure where to begin," Tessa

said, taking a sip of her drink.

"At the beginning usually works." Terry grinned at her.

"Well, what has my mother told you about the situation with her and my dad?"

"Bits and pieces," Terry said. "That he wasn't putting the effort in. That she felt neglected and lonely."

"Well, he just canceled his trip to Scotland to come back and sweep her off her feet, and she rejected him."

"Oh," Terry said. "Damn." He took a sip of his scotch.

"Yeah, tell me about it," Tessa said. She started telling the rest of the story, including how her mother was now staying at a hotel and her father was stuck alone in Tessa's apartment. She left out the stuff about her and Samson, for now. That was too heartbreaking to talk about.

"It seems to me," Terry said when she was finished, "that your mother needs a nice swift kick in the head to knock some sense into her."

"Are you volunteering?" Tessa asked with a smirk.

"Oh no," Terry said. "I'm the last person to give someone advice about relationships. I've never been in one. Spending so many years in jail got in the way of all that. But I do think it's a shame when someone like your mother takes what she has for granted. So maybe her marriage isn't perfect? No one's is. But at least she has a man who loves her. A man who, from the sound of it, spent most of his life providing for her and doing what he could. She says he didn't do 'enough.' Well, let me ask you this: What had your mother done?"

Tessa thought about that for a moment. Terry had a point. Her mother had been complaining for months that her father never did anything romantic. That he neglected her and made her feel lonely. But now, after he'd made this huge gesture, canceling his trip and flying back to make amends, her mother had not only rejected him, she had refused to put any effort into things herself.

When Dad had shown up at the apartment, her mother had complained that it "wasn't enough." But it seemed like her father was putting more effort into fixing things than her mother was. Maybe it "wasn't enough," but was it fair for him to have to do everything? When Mom was the one who had run out on him in the first place?

"You know," Tessa said, staring off to the side, "I spent the last six months listening to my mom's side of things. When I tried to talk to my dad, he said it was unfair to put it all on him, and that it was Mom's decision to leave. When I pressed him, he didn't seem to want to talk about it, so I let it drop."

"Well," Terry said, "to me it sounds like there's another side of the story there. I don't know your father, but I do know that a lot of the time, men, particularly older men like us, aren't so good at talking about what's bothering us. My father taught me that boys don't cry. That when something's wrong you man up and push through it." He made a thrusting gesture with his fist.

"Boys are expected to go out and get dirty, to bottle up their emotions inside and not deal with them. We don't get taught how to deal with our feelings. I had a lot of time over the years to think about the mistakes I made and where it all came from. And looking back on it now, I really believe that I wouldn't have made some horrible mistakes, if only I'd learned to better cope with the anger I had inside of me."

"So maybe my dad has something else going on?" Tessa asked, pursing her lips. "Mom kept saying that he was distant. That he wasn't spending enough time with her. I know he'd been working a lot of long hours. You think maybe there's something else there? Like, some reason he'd been like that?"

"I'd bet on it," Terry said. "Maybe what you need is to find out what's really going on with him, then get your mother to understand it. If she knew what was really going on with him, she might be more willing to forgive him."

Tessa nodded thoughtfully. "Yeah. Yeah, that makes sense. Thanks, Terry."

He raised his glass. "Any time, my dear."

Chapter Twelve

Tessa chatted with Terry over a few more drinks, before finally deciding it was time to head home and deal with the situation she'd been avoiding. When she arrived at home, she found her father sitting on the couch with a beer in his hand, watching TV. He looked up at her when she entered the apartment. "Hello, Tessa. I wasn't sure when you were coming home."

Tessa tossed her purse on the table and hung her jacket over the back of a chair. "Dad," she said, walking over and sitting next to him on the couch. "We need to talk."

"Of course, dear," he said, glancing briefly at her then looking back at the

TV.

Tessa picked up the remote and turned the TV off. "Dad, I'm serious."

He sighed and set his beer down on the coffee table. "All right, dear. What is it?"

"What's the real reason you've been so distant with Mom lately?"

He held up his hands helplessly. "I didn't think I had been. Tessa, your mother and I went over this time and time again before she moved out. She claimed I've been distant. That I've been ignoring her. But frankly, I don't know what she's talking about. I thought things were going just fine, until she started going on about feeling lonely. And then the next thing I knew, she was moving out."

"But there's got to be something else going on," Tessa said. "Maybe something you didn't do on purpose?"

He frowned. "Well, if I didn't do it on purpose, it's hardly fair for her to blame me for it, is it?"

Tessa sighed, leaning back against the couch. "I know, I know. But do you at least have an idea what it could be? What's been different lately?"

Dad shrugged. "I honestly don't know. She says I don't spend enough time with her. I told her it's not my fault I've been working late so much."

"Well, why have you been working late?" Tessa asked.

"We need the money," he said.

Tessa frowned. "What? Dad, you guys have never had trouble with money. Are you in debt or something?"

"Just the mortgage," he said. "But I need to get that paid off. When we sold the old house and bought our place down in Florida, we added a lot of time to our mortgage payments. I don't know how much you know about the housing market, but things were a lot cheaper when we bought the house you grew up in. Things are so much tougher these days."

Tessa thought about that. She really didn't know real estate—she hadn't planned to look into buying a house until after she got married someday—but she did know it was a lot more expensive to buy a house these days. She had assumed without really thinking about it that her parents' mortgage would be almost paid off. After all, they'd been married and working to pay for their home for nearly thirty years. Now that she thought about it, though, she realized that the added cost of a newer home in Florida could have extended her parents' mortgage by another five or ten years.

"I was hoping to retire someday, Tessa," Dad said. "I don't know if you noticed," he ran a hand through his gray, thinning hair, "but I'm getting up there in years. I turned sixty last year. Gonna be sixty-one a month from now. I'd like to retire when I'm sixty-five, hell maybe even sooner."

"But if you've got ten years left on the mortgage," Tessa said.

Dad shrugged. He took a swig of his beer. "Overtime helps a lot with that. I've been doubling up on some of the payments lately. Hell, more than that, since your mother moved out. I figure, if I keep it up, I can shave five years off the mortgage payments. Maybe be able to retire while I'm still young enough to enjoy it."

Tessa leaned her head against her hand, studying her father in a new light. "Have you tried talking to Mom about this?"

"About the mortgage?" He frowned at her. "Why would I? That's got nothing to do with this."

"Maybe it does," Tessa said. "Did you ever think that maybe, if she knew you were working so hard because you were worried about retirement and about paying off the house, she would have been more understanding? Heck, Dad, she told me once she thought you might be cheating because you were working so many long hours."

"I told you, Tessa, I would never. When I'm working late it's because I had a chance to pick up overtime."

"But you didn't tell Mom that."

He shrugged. "I thought she understood."

Tessa sighed. "Well, maybe it's about time you two sat down and talked about it. Maybe Mom will be more understanding when you tell her about the mortgage, and retirement, and all that. Maybe she won't feel so neglected if she knows you were doing all this for the sake of your future together."

Dad rubbed his chin. He shrugged. "Well, it's worth a shot. I guess I never thought about it that way."

"I'm going to call her," Tessa said. "See if she'll come over. Just to talk."

"All right. If you think it's a good idea.

J.L. STARR   469

Oh, by the way." He grabbed a piece of paper off the coffee table and handed it to her. "I almost forgot. Your boyfriend dropped by. Said if you changed your mind about tonight, this is where he'd be."

Tessa looked at the paper. There was an address written on it. She didn't recognize it specifically, but she knew it was in the downtown shopping area.

She bit her lower lip. She knew she had to go talk to Samson. It wouldn't be fair for her to tell her parents that they needed to talk things out if she weren't willing to do the same thing with Samson.

"All right," she said. "I'll go talk to Samson. And you have to talk to Mom."

"As long as she's willing to come down here and hear me out," Dad said, "I'd love to."

Tessa called her mother up. It took some convincing, but she managed to get her mother to agree to at least come and hear her father out. Tessa didn't know how the conversation would go, but if her parents were at least speaking to each other, she knew there was some hope.

When her mother arrived, Tessa waited only long enough to be sure that her parents would be civil to each other, then she left them to talk it out. She headed to her car and drove to the address Samson had left. She just hoped that when she got there, she and Samson would be able to find some common ground.

Chapter Thirteen

Tessa pulled into the parking lot at the address Samson had left. It was in a strip of businesses downtown, in an area filled with old, historic buildings, churches, law offices, and local government buildings. Interspersed up and down the road were a variety of little privately-owned businesses, from a flower shop to a tiny deli to a place that sold little homemade chocolates and candies, along with a handful of independently owned restaurants. It was exactly the sort of area Samson always preferred: filled with quaint, independent businesses instead of big corporate chains.

She parked in the small parking lot at

the end of the block, then walked up the street, checking the numbers on each storefront in search of the address. She went up and down the block twice before she realized that she'd walked past it each time. The place she was looking for, it seemed, was closed down. When she finally found what seemed to be the right door, it was for an abandoned shop. The lobby inside was empty of any furniture, with nothing but a couple of old paint cans and some stained drop cloths sitting in the center of the room. Above the door, where the old business's sign had once hung, there was nothing but the faded outline that showed where the business name had been before the sign was taken down.

Tessa checked the piece of paper again. The address listed was number 24-b, and that was where she was, but something was clearly wrong.

She was about to leave, while considering whether she should call

Samson, when a light went on in the back of the store.

Tessa stood up on her toes, trying to get a better look inside. The windows were dirty, but she thought she saw movement from somewhere in the back of the store.

Tessa knocked on the door. "Hello? Is someone in there?"

A moment later her phone chimed with a text message. It was from Samson: *Come inside.*

She texted him back: *What's going on?*

When she didn't get a response, she pulled the door open. It wasn't locked, so she stepped inside, looking around uncertainly. She felt a bit like an intruder. Why had Samson invited her to an abandoned building? She knew he could get up to some outside-the-box ideas at times, but spending New Year's Eve in an abandoned building wasn't exactly her idea of romantic.

She headed towards the back, looking around carefully with each step, afraid that she was going to be caught trespassing. When she got to the back room, she looked around for Samson, but he was nowhere to be found.

There was a small kitchen in the back room, filled with stainless steel commercial fixtures and ovens. There were a few bags and boxes sitting on one of the counters, and it looked like someone had been cooking. The smell of freshly cooked vegetables filled the room.

"Samson?" Tessa looked around, then she spotted a hall with a set of stairs leading up. There was an arrow, cut out of a piece of red construction paper, taped to the wall, pointing up the stairs.

She headed upstairs, finding an empty office with an old, abandoned desk. Another arrow taped to the desk pointed her down a hall to her left. She followed it past a bathroom and an old storeroom with empty shelves. At the end of the hall there was a ladder, leading up to a hatch in the roof. Another red arrow was taped to the wall by the ladder, pointing straight up.

"You've got to be kidding me," she said, looking up towards the hatch. It was open, revealing the darkening early-evening sky overhead.

She took a deep breath, then started climbing up the ladder.

When she got to the roof, what she saw took her breath away. Samson was standing in the middle of the roof, holding a single red rose. Next to him, there was a table covered in a white tablecloth. Covered plates of food sat on the table, along with a bottle of wine and two glasses.

"Samson?" Tessa stepped forward, looking over the scene with wide eyes. "What's going on?"

"I wasn't sure if you were still coming," he said, scratching the back of his head. "I've been planning this for awhile. And I guess that's why I lost my temper earlier, when it seemed like you were going to cancel."

Tessa swallowed a lump in her throat. "I don't understand." She gestured to the building below. "Why are we in an abandoned building?"

Samson handed her the rose, then held out a chair for her. She sat, looking out over the town. It was starting to get dark, and it was a bit chilly on the rooftop, but it was a beautiful sight.

"The building isn't exactly abandoned," Samson said, taking his seat. He pulled the lids off the plates in front of them, revealing a homecooked meal of vegetable lasagna, sauted baby vegetables, and stuffed zucchini.

"It looks abandoned," Tessa said, setting the rose down next to her plate. "There's nothing downstairs."

"Well, that's because the previous owner shut down six months ago."

Samson shrugged, a mischievous grin on his face.

"I don't understand," Tessa said.

"Well, remember when I said I was thinking of opening up my own business?"

Tessa stared at Samson, dumbstruck. Then her jaw dropped open. "You're kidding."

"Nope. I signed the lease papers last week." He opened the wine and poured them each a glass, then raised his in a toast. "Welcome to the Insert-Name-When-I-Pick-One Cafe and Tea Room. I'm still working on the name, of course. Do you think the INWIPO Cafe would be catchier?"

Tessa laughed, shaking her head. "Samson...you're absolutely crazy."

"Yeah, maybe." He shrugged. "But I figured, what the heck, right? I can't keep working the same job for the rest of my life. I got a small business loan, a menu I'm still working on, and about six months to make it work before I go bankrupt. Should be a blast."

"You're insane," Tessa said. She drank half of her wine in one sip. "So, this is why you invited me out here? To tell me you're taking a leap off the deep end into small business ownership?"

"Well, no," he said. "The real reason I asked you here was I wanted to show you what I bought at that jewelry store."

He reached across the table and pulled Tessa's napkin away, revealing a small velvet box underneath.

Tessa's heart leapt up into her throat. "Samson..."

"I know we hit a bit of a rough patch," he said. "But everybody hits those. I know we can work past it, and I want us to have a great future together."

Tessa picked up the box with trembling hands. She opened it and found a gold ring inside, shaped in the form of a flowering vine, with two tiny gold songbirds framing the diamond in the center. She couldn't breathe for a moment. She looked up at Samson with tears in her eyes.

"I thought..." she said.

"I know. It's okay."

She looked back down at the ring. She didn't feel like she deserved it. Not after the way she'd been treating Samson lately. The way she'd been so suspicious. She should have had more faith in him.

"So, what do you say?"

She looked up at Samson again, a smile slowly spreading across her lips. She nodded, too emotional to speak.

Samson pulled the ring from the box and slid it onto her finger. He held her hand, squeezing it tight.

"And now that you're in an agreeable mood," Samson said with a smirk, "there's one more thing I want to ask you."

"What else could you possibly ask me?" Tessa asked. Her head was spinning. She couldn't believe what was happening.

"Well, I'm going to need help running this place," he said. "I know it's not the fabulous corporate career path you had in mind, but I was hoping you'd work here with me. I could use a Quality Assurance Manager in the kitchen, after all."

Tessa swallowed a lump in her throat. The idea of quitting her job and helping run a business with Samson—with her future husband—was pretty scary. But as soon as she pictured it in her mind, it seemed perfect. No more corporate deadlines. No more tedious office work. She'd have the freedom of being her own boss. And when the weather grew warm again, she could grow watermelons in her garden and bring them down to the cafe to sell, along with the herbs for Samson's custom teas. It sounded absolutely perfect.

"I'll have to put in notice," she said.

"No rush," Samson said. "As you

might have noticed, the place isn't exactly ready to open yet."

They ate dinner together there on the rooftop, while Samson talked about all the ideas he had for how to run the place. They made plans to scour local thrift stores for cafe furniture, so that the decor would have a homey look instead of the plastic, artificial, commercialized look of most places these days. They talked about what it would be like, running the place together each day, setting their own hours and making all the big decisions on their own. And they talked about getting married and maybe one day, a few years down the road, starting a family together.

They talked until the rooftop grew too cold and the wine bottle was empty. Then they headed inside, leaving the dinner dishes in the kitchen for later. They drove back home to Tessa's apartment, and it wasn't until they opened the door that Tessa remembered that her parents were there.

As soon as Tessa and Samson walked in the door, her parents sat up on the couch, wearing guilty looks on their faces. They looked like a couple of teenagers who had just been caught when their parents came home.

"Well," Tessa said, tossing her purse on the table. "It looks like you two made up."

Her mother's face turned bright red. She adjusted her blouse, clearing her throat. "Ahem. Well, yes. No. Maybe. We...were talking things out."

"Damn right we were," Dad said with a wicked grin. Tessa's mother smacked him on the arm.

"Well, it's a good thing you're both getting along now," Tessa said. "Because we have news."

She held out her hand to show them the ring.

Her parents cheered the news,

offering their congratulations. Tessa's father shook Samson's hand, welcoming him to the family. Her mother started asking a million questions, wanting to know everything from how Samson popped the question to when the wedding would be. They sat and talked for hours, losing track of time, until they heard fireworks outside and realized that the new year had arrived.

With the hour so late, Tessa's parents got up to leave. "I already paid for my hotel room," her mother said. "We might as well make use of it. And besides, you lovebirds deserve your privacy."

Samson and Tessa's father shared a grin.

"What about tomorrow?" Tessa asked her mother. "Are you going back to Florida?"

Her parents exchanged a look. Mom said, "We'll see. Nothing's been decided yet."

But Tessa could see love in the way

her mother looked at her father. Maybe they still had issues to work out. But as long as the love was still there, she was sure they would make it work.

Her parents left, and Tessa and Samson settled down on the couch together. Samson put his arm around her. Tessa listened to the distant sound of the fireworks, while she sat there and admired her ring.

"You know what I just realized?" Tessa asked as she leaned against her fiance, snuggling close to him.

"What's that?"

"We have the apartment to ourselves," Tessa said. "For the first time in six months."

"It's a good feeling," Samson said.

Tessa snuggled tighter against him. "And it means you can finally move in."

"Well, I should hope so," Samson said with a grin. "I'd hate to still be living in my friend's basement after we're married."

"A spring wedding," Tessa said, starting to picture it. "Lots of flowers. But nothing extravagant. I like the idea of keeping it simple."

"I'm not wearing a suit," Samson said.

Tessa laughed. She pulled him close, kissing him dearly. She didn't want him to wear a suit. She'd be perfectly happy to see him standing at the altar in a pair of sandals and hand-woven pants. And she'd buy her dress at a little boutique from someone that sewed everything by hand. And it would be everything she could ever hope for.

She just had to promise herself one thing. That no matter what the future might bring, she'd be open and honest with him, and come to him when she had any worries or questions or concerns.

And, she promised herself: no more jumping to conclusions.

THE END

TESSA'S WINTER

About The Author

J.L. Starr lives in the country with her husband and their 2 rescue dogs. She can usually be found writing in her studio in the garden. Having spent the first 35 years of her life in the city, Starr finds the peace and solitude of the country to be the perfect place to bring the stories and characters in her mind to life.

Made in the USA
San Bernardino, CA
27 June 2019